Stardust Bound

Stardust Bound

a novel by karen cadora

Firebrand
Books
Ithaca, New York

Book design by Nightwood Design
Cover design by Lee Tackett

Printed in the United States on acid-free paper by McNaughton & Gunn

10 9 8 7 6 5 4 3 2 1

Library of Congress Cataloging-in-Publication Data

Cadora, Karen, 1970—
    Stardust bound : a novel / by Karen Cadora.
        p.   cm.
    ISBN 1-56341-053-2 (alk. paper). —ISBN 1-56341-052-4 (pbk. : alk. paper)
1. Women astronomers—Andes Region—Fiction.
2. Lesbians—Andes Region—Fiction.
    I. Title.
PS3553.A3144S73   1994
813'.54—dc20   94-29814
                                                       CIP

For Anne

1

It was raining. It was not supposed to rain in the Atacama Desert. No precipitation had been recorded in this region in years. Nevertheless, it was pouring sheets. I had not, of course, brought rain gear.

I had, however, brought a thermal parka. I got it out of my pack and put it on. Saskia had said that there could be snow higher up. Usually, it was just a dusting, but one year there had been a blizzard that kept the dome closed for an entire week. I just hoped that rain down here didn't translate into snow at the summit. Winter was not the best season for observing, but it was the only time it was cool enough to make this trek across the desert mountains.

It took me less than ten minutes to realize the parka was not going to work. I was boiling hot and drenched in sweat. I was as wet as if I'd let the rain fall on me. With a sigh and a half-hearted curse, I shrugged off my pack and stripped off the coat. I squatted down to rest.

"Shit!" I shrieked, leaping to my feet with more energy than I'd felt in several days.

I had been pricked by a barrel cactus. The small round balls of spines were practically the only vegetation in these barren hills. Of course I would sit on one. I sank down onto my pack, ready to cry. Everything was going wrong. I'd been hiking for three days, and there was still no sign of the observatory. If I hadn't seen the battered old sign by the road that used to be the Pan American Highway, back when people had cars, I would have written off the whole thing as just another one of Saskia's hallucinations. She'd been delirious at the end, her mind eaten up by drugs and cancer.

But the sign had been there, and I'd been able to make out the word *Observatorio*. Next to that were the words *La Vista*, and a faded array of the flags of all the countries of old Europe. Beyond the sign I'd found traces of a dirt road that branched out from the Pan American, making a beeline for the Andes. I had been following the road for two days now. If I didn't come upon the observatory soon, I was going to have to turn back. Even if my food supply was endless, which it wasn't, I was totally exhausted. The rec center had not prepared me for the relentless weight of the pack on my back across a hundred kilometers.

At least I could stop worrying about water. The dry land did not absorb the rain quickly, and tiny rivulets ran everywhere. I leaned over and filled my water purifier in one of the cleaner-looking ones. After a while, I dragged myself to my feet and began to climb again. The rain tapered off late in the afternoon, and I started to scout for a campsite. There was very little shelter to be had anywhere. Finally, I found a fairly flat spot barely off the road and pitched my tent. The sun broke through the clouds just before it set, a warm, brilliant flash of light. I stood there for a moment, appreciating the beauty.

I was about to turn back to my campsite when a flash of light in the east caught my eye. Not the west, where the sun was setting, but the east. My breath caught in my throat as I strained my eyes in that direction. There it was, on the peak rising just beyond the hill I was ascending—a small white-and-silver structure reflecting the last rays of sunlight. The dome. It had to be the dome at the observatory. The sun sank away, taking the traces of the dome with it, but I was sure of what I'd seen. I was within two days' hike now. A foolish grin took over my face, and I felt better than I had in months.

"We're going to make it," I said out loud.

This trip was all Saskia had talked about in the last few months. I could almost imagine her ghost hovering over me, smiling at me with approval. My humming was tuneless but cheerful as I made dinner and prepared for sleep.

When I woke, the sky was clear. I had a pang of regret. The night had probably been clear. I had missed my first chance to see the stars. My disappointment passed quickly, though, as I remembered the other sighting from the previous night. I was ready in record time, and I ate my breakfast as I hiked. The trail was relentlessly steep, and I gained nearly fifteen hundred meters in altitude. That night, I pitched my tent knowing that I was within half a day's walk of the dome. I slept soundly and woke early. My muscles ached, but I was eager to hike.

The tiny white dome flashed in and out of sight, bigger and bigger as I wound my way up the final peak. I hiked faster, ignoring the stitch in my side. This was no dream. The dome was there. It really was.

My eyes were locked on the summit, and my brain was full of starry dreams, so it did not immediately register that there was another person on the trail up ahead. For a moment, I thought I was imagining things. I hadn't seen a human being since I left New Serena days ago. People were not allowed to live outside New cities for fear they might damage the environment, and it was damned hard to get permission to go out-city even for a short time. I would never have been given permission if Saskia hadn't pulled strings. It was true, though, there was a human being approaching me and, I quickly realized, it was undeniably a woman. She had a pair of shoes knotted over her shoulder, but no backpack. I could not for the life of me figure out what she was doing out here.

"Hello," I called when she was close enough to hear.

The stranger just glared at me. She had piercing green eyes, and I could almost feel the anger pouring out of them. I opened my mouth to say something more, but the woman waved me silent.

"Get out of here," she growled.

Certainly not the most friendly of greetings. I told myself not to make too hasty a judgment. I, myself, had difficulty making favorable first impressions, so I tried to give even seemingly unpleasant strangers a fair chance.

"I'm from New Seattle," I said placatingly. "I'm looking for the observatory."

"I don't care where you're from. You're trespassing," the strange woman replied.

"Trespassing? Oh. What territory have I stumbled on?" I asked, still trying to sound cheerful.

"My territory," the woman replied scornfully, "so get out."

I was rapidly losing my sense of humor.

"Look here, you," I said, shrugging off my pack and letting it fall to the ground. "I've traveled five days through this damn desert to see the La Vista observatory, and no girl with an attitude is going to stop me."

The stranger did not immediately respond. I had a few moments to consider the possible consequences of antagonizing her. The woman was not as tall as me, but her thick forearms spoke of considerable strength. She was probably ten years my junior. Not a girl, no, but young enough to be insulted by the insinuation that she was. At least she didn't appear to be packing any weapons.

"How do you know about La Vista?" the woman asked eventually.

"I am here," I replied, equally cool, "at the behest of Dr. Saskia Rushkin."

"I knew it! Dr. Rushkin, indeed! Right on schedule. Where is the old bitch? Getting slow in her old age, is she?"

I felt something snap inside me. The flood of rage was hot and quick. I wanted to rip this stupid little chit to pieces, but some fragment of sense kept my fists at my side. She was probably stronger than I was, and certainly meaner.

"The *old bitch*," I said, the words like acid in my mouth, "is dead."

Her reaction was not the one that I had expected—the woman actually gasped.

"When?" she said in a strangled voice.

"A month ago," I replied, as coldly as I could. It was actually twenty-eight days to be exact, but I was trying not to count.

The words seemed to wilt the woman. She sank to the ground and covered her face with her hands. Just in case this was a bluff, I dug into my pack for my pocketknife. It wasn't much use as a weapon, but it made me feel better. I cautiously approached the stranger. She paid no attention to me. The obvious misery in those shaking shoulders was almost enough to make me feel sorry for her. Whatever problem this woman had had with Saskia, she had not wished her dead. At any rate, it did not seem wise to hang around. Here was a woman with a quick temper and a mean set of biceps. Prudently taking advantage of the break in hostilities, I hurried past the huddled form and continued up the trail. I looked over my shoulder frequently, but the stranger did not pursue me.

Two hours later, I rounded a sharp bend and found myself at the edge of the observatory. My jaw dropped in sheer amazement. There was not one dome, there were dozens, sprouting like a forest of mushrooms on the hillside. The dome I had seen from the trail was certainly the biggest, tens of meters across, but there were others scattered along the summit. Saskia hadn't told me there would be so many. I wandered among them. Each hemispherical dome was perched on top of a cool white column several stories high, and under each dome there was a scope—a telescope built to see the stars. They were relics from a previous century, a merciless, decadent, pleasure-seeking century, when billions starved while a few enjoyed the fruits of high tech, when there was money to spend on luxuries like stargazing.

Tentatively, I placed my hand against one of the columns. It really was there, at least seven meters tall. If the size of the dome was any indication, the telescope's mirror would be over a meter in diameter. With a mirror like that pointing at a clear sky, I could see to the edge of the galaxy and beyond. I closed my eyes at the thought. The breeze cooled the hot sting of tears on my face.

A sharp noise jolted me back to reality. I wiped my face on my sleeve. Gripping the knife in my pocket, I stepped out from behind the dome. Not far from where I stood, a dark, curly-headed man knelt outside a corrugated metal shack, tinkering with a gadget on top of a short pedestal. Another person. This abandoned observatory was turning out to be a virtual metropolis.

The man looked up at the sound of my footsteps.

"Hello," he said politely.

I stopped a few meters away, somewhat disconcerted by the friendly greeting. This one, at least, did not seem dangerous. He held a screwdriver in one hand and a small square mirror in the other.

"Bird shit," the man continued conversationally.

"What?" I asked, thoroughly taken aback.

It seemed that everyone on this mountain was unquestionably insane. I earnestly hoped that it wasn't a viral problem.

"Bird shit on the mirror," he explained. "Plays hell with your data. I was installing a replacement until I could clean this one up. So few birds, so much space, yet one of them just had to shit on my mirror."

"Oh," I said, edging closer to study the mirror that he held out for my inspection. "Is this some kind of telescope?"

"A solarscope," he corrected. "It's for studying the sun. That's why we only need a small mirror like this. Not like those monsters over there. The stars they're detecting are so small and far away that the mirrors have to be positively gigantic."

"Oh," I said again.

I was at a loss to say anything else. It was just too much to process all at once. I put a hand to my forehead.

"The altitude takes some getting used to," the man said sympathetically. "You might have headaches for a day or two. Anyway, welcome to La Vista. I'm Patrique."

I slowly let go of my knife and shook his hand.

"Quincy Alexander," I said.

"Quincy. Now why does that seem familiar?"

I shrugged. It was an unusual name, and I'd never met another with it.

"Ah," Patrique said triumphantly. "I've got it! Saskia Rushkin has a student named Quincy. Would that be you?"

"That's me," I said, surprised.

I put my hand back in my pocket and took hold of the knife again, just in case this man had the same feelings about Saskia as the woman on the trail had.

"Yes. She said she'd be bringing you on her next trip. Glad you could come. Is Saskia getting your stuff settled in the hotel?"

I studied the man for a moment. He had crooked teeth and friendly brown eyes.

"Have you been here long?" I asked.

"I've been here at La Vista for over three years now."

That surprised me a little. He looked healthy and well-fed, not like someone who'd been scrounging around in the desert for years. I studied his eyes. Even though I hardly knew him, I had a pretty good feeling about Patrique. He seemed like he had a heart.

"She died last month," I said gently. "It was very quick."

Patrique closed his eyes. I let go of my knife and patted him awkwardly on the arm.

"I mourn her loss," he said, after a pause. "She was a wonderful woman, and a great science administrator. She did so much for me. I'm greatly in her debt."

I nodded a little, feeling the familiar tightening in my throat.

"If you'd like," he added after a few moments of silence, "perhaps we could arrange a ceremony with the others."

"Others?"

I had been astonished to find two people up here. How many others could there be? Saskia had specifically said that this was an abandoned observatory. *Abandoned,* the last time I checked, meant no people. I cleared my throat and asked for an explanation.

"There are about fifty of us here at any one time. I'm one of a few permanent people. The rest come on their vacation time. We're pretty much self-supporting. You're welcome to stay as long as you want. I'll show you around."

In a daze, I followed the man around the summit. Besides the telescopes, there was an enormous greenhouse, a solar generator, and a well. Beyond the greenhouse, there was a large building that Patrique called the hotel. It had living quarters, common rooms, and eating facilities. Patrique showed me into an empty bedroom on the second floor. I dropped my bags and looked around in amazement. There was a double bed with sheets and blankets, an easy chair, and even a small computer terminal. I strode over to the window. The view of the mountains was incredible. In the distance, I could see the snow-capped peaks in the highest part of the Andes.

"We try to minimize light pollution," Patrique said, "so keep your shades down at night. Excess light disturbs the observations. Do you have a flashlight? Good. You'll need it to get around after dark. Also, we all do chores—maintenance, cleaning, cooking, whatever. We usually work for an hour or two right after dinner. Talk to Carla tonight, and she'll fit you into the schedule."

I nodded dumbly, struck by how odd it was to be in a place where darkness was so precious that light was considered pollution.

Patrique took me through the rest of the facilities. There was even a shower room with hot and cold running water. I had thought I'd be living in a tent and eating dried protein bars, but there was nothing primitive about this place.

"The other astronomers..."

I felt shivers go down my spine when Patrique said that word. Real live astronomers.

"...observe at night and sleep during the day. They usually wake up around sunset. I'm a day person myself, since I'm observing the sun. We all try to eat dinner together, though. They'll be stirring shortly, I should think."

We sat in the dining room. Patrique boiled water for tea and brought out some cookies left over from the night before.

"I am overwhelmed," I remarked. "This isn't what I was expecting at all."

"And what were you expecting?" Patrique asked with a grin.

He obviously loved showing off La Vista and relished my amazement.

"Well, in the first place, after I encountered your guard, I thought I was going to have to fight my way in here."

Patrique looked at me blankly.

"Guard? What guard?" he asked.

I described my encounter with the woman on the hill.

"Short brown hair, green eyes?" Patrique asked.

"That's the one."

She had been very striking, too, I realized suddenly, with those strong, sharp features accenting her piercing eyes. That observation had not crossed my mind earlier. It was much easier to think about such details when I wasn't in immediate danger of getting my ass kicked.

"That was Rubie Marle," Patrique said with a sigh. "She's a bit, well, protective of these mountains."

"Protective? That's an understatement."

"Well, Rubie isn't an astronomer. She's a hiking and rock-climbing fanatic. She hangs out at La Vista between trips. It's hard for her to appreciate the work we do. She doesn't understand why we come up here at all. She's afraid we're going to pollute everything."

"I thought she was going to assault me," I said.

Patrique sighed again.

"She's got a pretty quick temper, Quincy, and she's not the easiest person to understand. But give her a second chance. She's a good person at heart."

"But what about her reaction to Saskia's death? That was definitely weird."

"I didn't know they knew each other," he said with a shrug.

Before I could ply him with more questions, two new people came in. They were bleary-eyed from sleep. Patrique poured tea for them.

"Welcome aboard, Quincy," Martine said, after we'd been introduced. "Nice to see a fresh face."

Martine was a big, beautiful woman from New Domingo. She was probably in her sixties, and her close-cropped black hair was fading to gray. Although I'd never met her before, I knew a little about her. She and Saskia had worked closely together in the first stages of the Reconstruction. They hadn't been good friends—colleagues was the word Saskia used—but Saskia had respected Martine, and that was quite enough for me to adore her. Yet none of the stories Saskia had told me about Martine's scientific prowess prepared me for the woman herself: she was absolutely charming.

Carla grunted a greeting as she hunched over her tea. From the affectionate tussle Martine gave her hair, I guessed that the two of them were lovers. I was very pleased to learn that both Martine and

Carla were permanent residents at La Vista. That certainly boded well for the place. I hoped that the presence of these two would more than make up for the bristly Rubie. The four of us chatted quite amiably for a while.

"Hey," Patrique said, after hearing that I trained at UniTech's New Sydney labs, "you didn't know Cassandra Hower, did you? She trained there too."

"I knew her," I said slowly, "extremely well."

"Isn't that something? Her family lived next door to us for years. How is she? She used to be one sharp and sassy girl."

"She still is," I said quietly.

I did not want to talk about Cass. Just then, Martine chimed in with a completely different topic. I caught her eye and gave her a small nod of gratitude. The little smile wrinkles on her face puckered with equal parts of comprehension and compassion.

After a while, Patrique went off to clean his mirror, and Carla and Martine started the evening meal. I followed them into the kitchen and peeled potatoes while they told me many of the ins and outs of the observatory.

The rest of the crew tromped in to sit down to vegetable stew, biscuits, and rhubarb pie. I felt very welcome and comfortable, and the reason soon dawned on me: I was sitting in a room full of women. I was astonished to see that Patrique was the only man present. The astronomers were a diverse group, hailing from dozens of the New cities in the world, and they all were women. I chewed on this realization along with my food. It must have been Saskia's doing. She had been the first person to rediscover La Vista over twenty years ago. Perhaps she had discouraged men from coming here. She had never struck me as particularly woman-centered, but it seemed like the best explanation. I was greatly pleased with the idea that she'd reserved this starry haven for women.

Toward the end of the meal, Rubie slipped in and took a place down the table. I kept a wary eye on her, but she completely ignored me. She said hello to several people and ate heartily.

Cleaning up was a communal affair. When the dishes were washed and the food put away, everyone came back to the table. I had been figuring out where all the dishes went, so there was only one chair vacant when I hurried into the dining room. I was seated before I realized that Rubie was directly to my left. The hairs on my arms prickled. I crossed my legs and leaned to the right. Chairs shifted as everyone got comfortable and the room grew quiet.

"New duty roster coming out tomorrow," Carla started. "Please check it out. And Francoise and Theresa are heading out at the end of the week, so don't forget to wish them well."

"Party at my place Thursday night," Francoise interjected. "BYO whatever."

"Oh," Theresa injected, "speaking of my departure, I need someone to go over the hydraulics in the greenhouse with me. I fixed the bug, but you'll have to do some minor maintenance while I'm away to keep it running properly."

"I can handle it," said Martine. "Just show me what to do before I go out to the scope tonight."

Theresa thanked her. When everyone else was done with their announcements, Patrique stood up.

"Last, but not least, the new face among us is Quincy Alexander, Saskia Rushkin's student from the New Seattle labs. Did you want to say anything to the group, Quincy, about Saskia, perhaps?"

I nodded and cleared my throat. Patrique had told me earlier that Saskia Rushkin was well-known among the group. She had been, after all, the founding mother of La Vista. He had offered to make this announcement, but I wanted to do it myself. I leaned forward to rest my forearms on the table.

"Saskia," I said finally, "wanted very much to be here this winter. We had planned to come together. When it became clear that she was terminally ill, she made me promise that I would go alone. She requested that I take her ashes with me."

There was a long silence. Rubie, sitting next to me, had gone completely rigid.

"How did she die?" someone asked softly.

"VBC," I said. "It was incredibly fast, incredibly virulent. She died before they could engineer a cure."

"How the hell did she get viral brain cancer?" asked Francoise.

She was angry. I understood. I was angry, too. The Second Catastrophe was over. There weren't supposed to be any virals, or at least not any that our IMCs couldn't handle.

"It appears she contracted it when she was young and that it remained dormant for sixty years or more."

"How contagious is it?" Theresa said, a little anxiously.

Her anxiety was understandable. Many of these peoₗ
in contact with Saskia for years.

"Hardly at all," I said reassuringly. "Apparently it's cued tₗ
specific blood type. A very rare blood type, too. At any rate, the
code was keyed into MedCen last week, so everyone's IMC has beₗ
updated."

Internal Medical Computers were perhaps the only reason anyone
survived the virals from the Second Catastrophe. These tiny computers were installed at birth, placed under the skin on the inner arm. An
access port near the thumb allowed an individual's IMC to interface
with the huge machines at Medical Central whose data bases were
packed full of the codes of all known virals. Interacting with the immune system, an IMC was capable of genetically engineering vac-
cines and cures from inside the body itself.

"But many of us have been here at La Vista for more than a few
weeks," Patrique said gravely.

"And you don't have access to the Net?" I asked, astonished. In
New Seattle, just passing my hand through the ID scanner, whether
it was to open a lock or log on to the mainframe, would update my
IMC. I fully expected to have access at a facility as sophisticated as
this.

Patrique shrugged.

"The last I checked, astronomy was still a crime," he said. "UniTech
is not in the habit of offering Net access to science criminals."

"Oh," I said, a little abashed. It was stupid of me to have forgotten
that. "Well, do you have one of those medical servers?"

A medserver was like a portable electronic hospital. It could diag-
nose and dispense IMC code for a huge number of injuries and dis-
eases. While it couldn't actually set bones or perform surgery, it did
almost everything else.

"Of course," Martine said. "We use it all the time."

"Then I should be able to transfer the codes from my IMC to the
medserver and test all of you from there. If anyone needs the cure, I
can transfer that code too."

"Well, why don't you start," Carla suggested, "and we'll all get tested
before we go out to the scopes tonight. Everyone will feel better. If
you need any help, ask Martine. She's our doctor in residence."

The others dispersed to their chores. Patrique brought the medserver
and a well-stocked electronics kit up to the dining room. I thanked

him before turning to my work. One look at the server told me that constructing an interface for my IMC would not be hard, so I got out the e-tweezers and a baseboard and started to build. Patrique hovered a little, offering his assistance. When he was called off on another errand a few minutes later, I breathed a sigh of relief. Men need so much attention sometimes that it's hard to concentrate when they're around. Besides, I was beginning to suspect that Patrique's attentions were not completely platonic. The last thing I needed was some hormonal male making passes at me. I'd have to set him straight sometime in the near future. The trick was to do it gently. He wasn't a bad guy, and I didn't want to hurt his feelings. I just wanted him to direct his interest elsewhere.

Some time later, the sensation of being hovered over returned. I sighed inwardly. It looked like the near future was getting nearer. At least Patrique had chosen a good moment to reappear. I didn't want to let go of the circuit component I was holding, but I needed the magnetic welder and it was just out of my reach.

"Would you mind passing the m-welder over here?" I asked without looking up.

The handle was immediately placed in my hand. I thumbed the switch and made the weld. I reached for another circuit switch with my e-tweezers, hoping that if I appeared to be completely absorbed in my work, Patrique would leave me alone.

"How's it going?" asked a most un-Patrique-like voice.

Any tech worth her wits knows better than to let herself be distracted while she's holding a component. It would have taken hours to find if I dropped it. So I set the component in the baseboard and pretended to fuss a little over its positioning, which gave me an extra moment to adjust to the fact that it was Rubie, not Patrique, standing beside me.

"Fine," I said, meeting her gaze ever so briefly.

Rubie seemed to take that as permission to sit down across from me, because that's what she did. I swallowed, a little nervous. At least she wasn't holding a large knife or anything like that.

"So this is your first time at La Vista," she said casually.

Again, only my years of training prevented me from dropping my e-tweezers. The last thing I expected from Rubie was casual chitchat. Evidently, she had decided to strike up a conversation. This was an interesting turn of events, and I took it as a good sign. If Rubie was talking, she was probably less likely to be planning murderous deeds.

"Yes," I replied, not letting my surprise show. "And you?"

"The same. And how are you enjoying it so far?"

I couldn't believe it. Here was a woman I'd almost come to blows with just a few hours earlier, mouthing the formalities of polite conversation. It was definitely disorienting.

"Well, almost everyone has been very...," I paused so that I could look at her face, "...welcoming."

Rubie actually winced at that. I hurriedly looked back at my work. Although I hated to admit it, that little dig felt great.

"I'm glad to hear it," she said finally, sounding almost humble. "They're a great group of people from what I've seen."

Suddenly, I understood what was happening. Rubie was trying to apologize. It was, I realized with sadness, something that Saskia would do. Saskia was quick to lose her temper, and it was hard for her to apologize outright, even when she knew herself to be in the wrong. Sorry was not a word in her vocabulary. So she would just go out of her way to be polite and contrite afterward. It appeared that Rubie had a similar strategy.

"Be careful of Patrique, though," Rubie added. "He's kind of a scammer."

I turned back to my circuit.

"How so?" I asked.

"He tries to bed all the new ones, especially the tall, pretty ones like you," Rubie warned.

I chuckled. "Does he? He's in for a disappointment then."

"It won't be for lack of trying on his part. Those soft doe eyes of his bring them down like flies."

I looked up. Rubie's face was more relaxed now. It wasn't what I'd call a smile, but it was a pleasant change from her earlier grimace. Suddenly Rubie looked up, too, and I found myself staring straight into her bright eyes.

"Patrique?" I joked lightly. "But he has such funny teeth. And he probably has hair on his back."

"For the compulsively hetero woman," Rubie replied, "La Vista has pretty limited resources. After a week or two, Patrique starts to look pretty good."

"Not to me," I said firmly, adding a little shudder for effect.

"What? Are you taken?" Rubie asked, her voice almost playful.

I jerked my eyes back down to my baseboard. That was twice in one night that someone had reminded me of Cass.

"No. Not any more."

"Oh. That's too bad," Rubie said, with a hint of real sympathy in her voice.

I didn't want to pursue the topic, so I asked Rubie to help me. An extra pair of hands was actually quite useful. Even though she didn't know anything about hardware, she could hold the baseboard and align the light fibers while I made a few adjustments.

"Anyway, I shouldn't be too hard on old Patrique," Rubie continued, after we'd been working in silence for a few minutes. "He can be a good friend."

"Even if I reject him as a lover?" I asked.

"Especially if you reject him as a lover," Rubie replied with mischief in her voice.

We shared a grin at the truth of that.

"Huh," I snorted as I poked at the fiber. "Boys."

"Yeah, you can have 'em."

"Not in my bed," I said emphatically.

"Oh, a purist," Rubie said.

She was definitely teasing me.

"Yeah, well," I shrugged. "I know what I like. There it is, that should do it."

I put my tools down and laid the interface fiber across my wrist port.

"See any adhesive in the kit?" I asked.

A standard interface automatically kept the light beam focused on the access port, but this hack job wasn't going to do any tricks like that. I studied Rubie as she taped the interface to my wrist. At first, I had been wary of her friendly overtures. Our first encounter was still fresh in my memory. As we'd continued to talk, however, I'd felt my reservations crumbling. Rubie was young, and a lot of what I found abrasive about her could be chalked up to immaturity. I decided to give the crusty little thing another chance.

"How's it going?" Patrique asked, poking his head in the room.

I dared not look at Rubie, because I knew I'd start giggling.

"Great," I said. "We were just going to call in volunteers. You can be the first patient. It takes about twenty seconds."

Rubie grabbed his arm and propelled him into the room.

"I'll call the others," she said, offering Patrique her chair.

"You two are getting along better," Patrique said when Rubie was gone.

"Yeah, we are," I said. "Thanks for telling me to give her a second chance."

Patrique tested negative for the virus, as did everyone else who filed through the room. I updated everybody's IMC anyway—you never knew where a viral could be lurking.

"I almost forgot about you, Rubie," I said, when the dining room was empty again. "Sit down."

I stripped the interface off my wrist while the test ran. My head snapped up at the sound of the medserver alert.

"I'll be damned," I said, looking at the screen. "You've got it. Sit still. I'm going to program your IMC with the disinfectant procedures."

I strapped the interface into her wrist access port, and tapped the transfer protocol into the keyboard. I studied the test results while the procedure ran.

"Huh," I said, peering at the screen. "You have the blood type that's so susceptible to this virus. Very unlucky. Literally, there's about one in ten thousand chance of that."

I looked up. Rubie was extremely pale, her eyes blank. She looked terrified.

"Hey, Rubie, look here at me," I said quickly. "It's okay. You hear me? Don't get freaked out about this. In about a minute, your IMC's going to be pumping out antivirals by the pint. You'll be clear in a few days, no question about it."

Rubie blinked. I reached out and patted her hand. It was clammy.

"You're safe," I said. "You hear me? You almost certainly would have been fine even if it had gone undetected for years. This is a very long-term thing."

The medserver beeped. The procedure was complete. I detached the access and powered the machine down.

"Of course, you're right," Rubie said, slowly. "Thank you, Quincy."

I patted her hand again. This time, Rubie held onto me for a moment. Her eyes were losing their frightened look. I smiled reassuringly and nodded toward the medserver.

"I'll leave this hooked up and we can run another test in the morning so you won't be worried about it."

I squeezed Rubie's hand and got an answering squeeze. Rubie's rough and calloused hand was a pleasant contrast to my long, science-smooth fingers. Where did this woman get such hands? Climbing, I guessed. I gave Rubie another squeeze and let go.

"Great," Rubie said as she stood up. "Thanks. In the meantime, I think I'll take a walk to clear my head. Would you like to come?"

I shook my head regretfully.

"I'd like to, Rubie, but Martine offered to take me up to her scope tonight, and I don't want to miss a minute of astronomy. This place is so incredible. Now I understand why Saskia wanted so badly for me to see it. I'm glad she made me promise to come."

I was not prepared for Rubie's reaction. She turned on her heel and headed for the door without another word. There was anger in every taut line of her body.

"Rubie, wait."

She paused half a step before continuing her march. I started to get up and go after her.

"Rubie, really, I didn't mean to be so tactless. I'd love to go for a walk with you. Just not tonight. Okay?"

She stopped barely long enough to jerk open the door.

"Whatever," she said coldly.

She was gone. The door slammed shut. I stood there, immobilized. I had no idea what had just happened: Rubie had turned back into the belligerent woman I'd met on the trail.

★

A few minutes later I went in search of Martine. Having recovered somewhat from Rubie's abrupt departure, I was once again burning with enthusiasm for the night's activities. It was still early, so I headed downstairs to the greenhouse. Martine had said she'd be there with Theresa for at least a couple of hours after dinner.

"Over here, Quincy," Martine shouted from the far side of the greenhouse.

Theresa and Martine were hunched over a large water pump. I wound my way down the aisles toward them, passing a few people who were busy tending the plants. I smiled and nodded, unsure of names.

"How'd it go with the viral tests?" Theresa asked.

"Only one positive," I said cheerfully, "and that'll be clear in a few days."

"Rubie?" Martine asked from behind a tank.

"Well, yes," I said, puzzled. "How did you guess?"

Martine just stared at me for a moment.

"Just lucky," she said finally.

I couldn't fathom that one, so I let the subject drop. I asked instead about the greenhouses and was rewarded with a barrage of information about lighting cycles and temperature control. I nodded politely, trying not to yawn. I'd come here to see the stars.

Martine and Theresa quickly finished up their work. The three of us left together. As they walked down the corridor toward the stairs, Jin-Li, a fusionist from New Singapore, passed us at a jog.

"What's the hurry?" Martine asked.

"It's the clearest night I've seen since I've been here," Jin-Li said with a grin.

"Interferometric?" Theresa asked eagerly.

"No doubt."

Theresa whooped and started running after Jin-Li. Martine laughed.

"What's that all about?" I asked.

"Oh, the weather's been unbelievably bad these last few weeks. You can still do some kinds of observing if it's a little hazy or cloudy, but interferometry needs near-perfect conditions. Those kids have been cooling their heels for days, waiting for the sky to clear."

"And you?"

"I'm updating a star catalog. All you need is enough light to measure the Doppler shift. I'm not resolving any images, so I can still work if the viewing is less than perfect. Of course, there've been several nights recently when even I couldn't do it. Can't see through clouds, you know. At least my scope can't."

"Are there scopes that can?" I asked eagerly.

Now, that would be an impressive machine.

"Back in its heyday, the radioscope worked around the clock, through sun and clouds. Radio signals are much more robust than visible or infrared. Patrique's been talking about trying to get it running again."

Something in Martine's voice told me that she didn't think the project was worthy of that kind of attention.

"You disapprove?" I asked.

"Well, I think it's a waste of time. The damn thing is too complicated for us. It's like the five-meter NTS."

"NTS?"

"New Tech Scope. The huge one at the very top of the hill that you can see from miles away. It was the cutting edge when it was built, oh, almost seventy years ago. New equipment, new theories. In some ways, it was almost as good as many of the space telescopes. It gave us the first really conclusive evidence of black holes."

Black holes. The words made my skin tingle. When Saskia had first told me about them years ago, I hadn't believed her. Collapsed stars so dense, even light couldn't escape from their gravitational pull. They were too fantastic. And nobody had ever mentioned them in school. But then Saskia worked the theory out, showed me the data, made me believe in them.

"How can you think that's a waste of time?" I asked. "I mean, black holes are the most incredible things. That's what astronomy is all about."

Martine sighed deeply. We reached the top of the stairs and headed down another corridor to the sleeping quarters. The temperature outside plunged when the sun went down, and we were going to pick up my parka from my room. We were at my door before Martine answered the question.

"Black holes are incredible, Quincy. I love to think about them. That's why we're all here instead of at some cushy UniTech vacation center. The images and ideas of astronomy make our lives much richer. But it's mostly a matter of economics. There are so few of us, and we have so little time.

"When the NTS was up, it had ten technicians and three astronomers working full-time to keep it going. Trucks came here daily with parts, supplies, food. That took a lot of money. Now that money goes to UniTech and the Reconstruction—to making the air breathable, curing the virals, and building clean New cities."

I nodded. Much as I loved the stars, I did not disagree with what the United Technologies Corporation had done. Fifty years ago, the earth had been dying. The First Catastrophe had turned Eastern Europe into a molten nuclear zone. Out of this wasteland came the mutant virals of the Second Cat. In less than five years, they had cut the world's population in half. The Third Cat killed billions more: the downright criminal pollution and destruction of Earth's natural resources had been going on for centuries, but no one fully realized the consequences of such behavior until it was far too late. By commandeering every available technological resource and committing them exclusively to the Reconstruction, UniTech had undeniably saved humanity from extinction. There were, at present, only about a hundred million people in the safety of UniTech's fifty or so New cities. That was all that remained of the human race. La Vista had died, but Earth lived. It seemed like a fair trade, even to a star fanatic like me.

I shrugged on my parka and got my gloves. We left my room and started heading back down the corridor.

"Humanity can't afford luxuries like astronomy," Martine continued. "One day, we will be able to. Until then, we have to concentrate on doing the work that our resources allow. And that means small scopes, short projects. We can do valuable work without doing big, fancy things. There's no way we can run the NTS by ourselves right now."

"Of course, you're right," I said. "It's just that, well, I don't know. It's just a little disappointing."

We had reached the door to the outside. I stepped through, absorbed in our conversation. Martine came after and shut the door behind us.

"You're disappointed?" Martine said, her voice full of amusement. "My dear, have you looked up recently?"

I looked up and gasped.

"Oh, God," I whispered, incredulous. "I don't believe it."

It was full dark and the sky was unspeakably brilliant with stars. Millions of them. Radiant, explosive, precious. The stuff of dreams. I spun around. They were everywhere. I was enclosed in a cup of stars, drinking in the night. I stared and stared, burning the sight into memory.

"Careful," Martine said, grabbing my arm to steady me.

Dizzy and swaying, I leaned gratefully against Martine.

"Am I delirious?" I asked, still staring at the sky.

"Probably," Martine replied. "It would be hard not to be."

"Where," I paused for a moment to recollect my readings, "where's the Southern Cross?"

"For all its fame, it's actually very small," Martine commented as she pointed it out. She directed my gaze to more impressive constellations.

"What about the Magellanic Clouds?"

"Well, the large one hasn't risen yet. You can see it if you come out around 2:00 or 3:00 A.M. The small one is just over there on the horizon. See?"

"The fuzzy thing that almost looks like a cloud?"

"That's it."

"Huh," I said, unimpressed.

Martine laughed. She had a sunny, rolling chuckle.

"Yeah. It's kind of pathetic, I know. Just try to remember how far away it is. Then it will seem more impressive."

"Outside the galaxy," I mused. "You know, I just can't fathom that kind of distance."

Martine chuckled again.

"I don't know if anyone can, Quincy. What's a hundred thousand light years and more to mortals like us?"

I reached back to rub the crick in my neck. My eyes hurt with the beauty of it all.

"I just wish Saskia were here," I murmured. "So many things make sense now."

"She really kept the place lively. Loud voice, quick temper, and no tolerance for bullshit."

"Yeah," I said. "That was her all right."

"Come on," Martine said, after a moment. "Let's go up to my scope before we freeze to death out here."

We didn't need flashlights. The starlight alone was enough to light the way. We hiked up the hillside. Martine led us to one of the medium-sized domes.

"This observatory was built by a federation of European countries. The scope was made by the Danes. The main mirror is 1.2 meters in diameter," Martine told me as she opened the door.

We ascended two flights of stairs before coming to the control room. Martine explained the workings of the main computer bank as she initialized the observing program and opened the dome. The procedure itself was quite simple, and the computers did most of the difficult work.

"This list of stars," Martine said, pointing to a huge book, "was cataloged about seventy years ago. I'm going back through them and noting down any changes that might have occurred since then."

"In hopes of finding what?" I asked as Martine punched in the coordinates of a star.

Martine shrugged, flicked a few toggles and sat back as the computers positioned the scope to the right part of the sky.

"Anything different," she said. "For example, suppose this star is actually part of a binary star system and that seventy years ago, the other star was hidden behind it. Or suppose this star has undergone a cataclysmic change. That would show in the spectrum."

I sat next to Martine, talking astronomy and helping her record the data. I was very happy. I had not had anyone to talk to like this except Saskia. Just talking about astronomy was not in itself illegal. You could only get arrested for doing it on the Net. Illegal appropriation of Reconstruction resources for nonessential science was a big no-no. Talking was fine. Still, no one else at UniTech seemed even remotely interested in discussing the topic. No one else got the same surge of excitement talking about pulsars, nebulae, variable stars, and interstellar dust. In fact, most people didn't even know how many planets there were in the solar system, much less what their names were.

"Okay," Martine said after a moment. "That's it for this section. I'm going to rotate the dome so we can look at a different part of the sky. Do you want to go up and watch? It's kind of fun to watch the equipment move."

"In the dome?" I said excitedly.

"Yes. Go through that door up there and up the stairs. There's a catwalk around the scope that you can walk on."

I was up in a flash.

"Be sure to close the door behind you," Martine called after me. Her warm chuckle followed me up the dark stairs.

I paused at the top of the stairs, waiting for my eyes to adjust. It was cold up here. Soon I could make out the dim outline of the scope. It was in the center of the room, pointed at the opening in the dome overhead. Considering the size of the dome, the scope itself seemed small, perhaps only three meters high. Of course, the electronics that controlled the thing were in the rooms downstairs.

A loud clanging noise made me jump. Up above, the dome was starting to move. I sat down quickly on the catwalk and looked up. The patch of stars that was visible through the opening in the dome's ceiling had begun to rotate. For a moment, I was queasy. I told myself sternly that only the dome was moving, not the ground. Still, I felt much better when the motion stopped.

A whir of machinery indicated that the mirror was shifting, focusing a star on its optical system. It stayed like that for perhaps twenty seconds, soaking up the starlight. Downstairs, Martine was recording the peak in the spectrum. Then the mirror moved again.

I laid down on the catwalk and looked up at the stars. It was comforting that there was only a small portion of the sky visible at one time. It wasn't as overwhelming as being out beneath the whole blazing firmament.

A hand on my shoulder shook me awake.

"What?" I said, sitting bolt upright.

I was stiff with cold. Martine was kneeling beside me.

"You fell asleep, dear. Why don't you go to bed? It takes a day or two to get your body on the observing schedule. In the meantime, we don't want you getting hypothermia."

"What time is it?" I asked blearily.

"Almost two-thirty," Martine said, pulling me up. "Time for you to be in bed. Do you have your flashlight? Can you find your way back to your quarters?"

I held up the flashlight and said good-bye. A breeze had kicked up, and as I stumbled down the hill to the hotel, the extent of my exhaustion became clear. The long hike to La Vista had taken a lot out of my body. When I reached my room, I tumbled into bed without undressing and was immediately asleep.

2

It was dark when I woke. My internal clock told me it was late morning, but there was no light. Just before I drifted back to sleep, I realized that the shades on the windows kept the light out completely. It would be dark inside no matter what time of day it was.

When I woke the next time, I stumbled through the dark to where I thought the window was. After some fumbling, I found the cord and lifted the shade. That was a mistake. I sat down on the windowsill and closed my eyes against the blazing sunlight. Bit by bit, I was able to open them. It was full daylight, probably afternoon.

It took me a while before I stood up. I was incredibly stiff. A hot shower was what I needed, and with a grin, I remembered that there was one only a few steps away. I gathered my things and headed upstairs. The showers were empty. It was too early for the astronomers to be up and about, and Patrique had probably gotten up at dawn to start the solarscope.

I luxuriated in the hot spray of water. It had been days since I'd bathed. I soaped up twice, scrubbing my skin with a sponge I found in the cabinets outside. It felt so good. I rolled my neck and bent over to touch my toes, letting the water pound the soreness out of my back and legs.

When I emerged from the shower, the entire room was opaque with steam. I toweled off and got dressed. There was empty space on some of the shelves, so I put my toiletries there and hung my towel on an unclaimed hook.

Instead of returning to my room, I stopped at the kitchen for a bite to eat. I made tea and toast. The bread was excellent. Nightly bread-making was one of the chores on Carla's list. Of course, the bread machines in the kitchen made it a simple procedure, but that didn't detract from the taste at all.

"Hi, Quincy."

I turned to see Patrique coming into the dining hall.

"Hey, what's up?"

"Just coming in for lunch," he said, passing into the kitchen. "Let me make a sandwich and I'll be right there."

I got up to make some more tea. Patrique asked me about my first night, and we talked amiably about observatory life for a few minutes.

"Rubie's viral is clearing out nicely," Patrique mentioned. "I helped her run a test first thing this morning."

"Good. I'm glad," I replied. "I know she was a little concerned about it. It's probably a load off her mind."

So Rubie had confided in Patrique. I wondered what else she passed along. Just how close were those two? The tiny stab of jealousy accompanying that thought took me by surprise.

"She likes you," Patrique said.

Luckily, my mouth was full, and I was prevented from making an immediate and almost assuredly undignified response. I swallowed carefully.

"Really?" I asked nonchalantly.

"She told me so this morning. She said you were very sweet."

It looked like Rubie had gotten over whatever snit possessed her last night.

"I just hope that means she's going to take me off her hit list," I joked lightly, but the sentiment was dead serious. Rubie had gone from being warm and friendly to prickly cold in less than a minute. It was hard to be friends with someone on a hair trigger.

"So," Patrique said, leaning across the table, "we have a mutual acquaintance. Tell me, really, how is Cassandra? I haven't seen her for more than seven years."

I felt my heart sink as he spoke. He had clearly not picked up on my reluctance to discuss that topic. Still, I thought, talking about Cass might enable me to discourage Patrique's romantic inclinations without having to reject him outright. I gritted my teeth and dove right into the middle of it.

"Well, I don't really know how she is these days," I said. "She broke up with me several months ago."

"Oh," Patrique said, taken aback. "I'm sorry to hear that."

"Yeah, I was too," I replied. I did not have to fake the bitterness in my voice. "She ran away with an oceanologist. They're somewhere in the middle of the North Atlantic."

"Oh," Patrique said again.

"It has been a pretty miserable year for me," I continued. "My lover of two years dumped me, and my best friend and mentor died of a freak viral."

"Oh," Patrique said yet again, but this time he put real sympathy into the word. "You must be feeling terribly lost."

He was actually coping rather well. Patrique was probably accustomed to being rejected on account of his gender. Even my limited knowledge of La Vista's inhabitants was enough to assure me that a sizable proportion of them were substantially queer.

"Lost, yes, that's a good word. The two people I loved most, gone, just like that. Cass alone I could've handled. I always knew she'd leave some day. But Saskia. God, sometimes I wish I'd died instead of her."

Patrique gave me the gift of silence, for which I was grateful. I stared into my teacup.

I'd been nineteen when I'd met Saskia. I was a junior student in eco-engineering, hellbent on the Reconstruction. My interest was in atmospheric recovery. In fact, my senior project ended up being the basis for the large-scale air filters I designed for New Tucson. At any rate, the school required several courses outside the major. So I very reluctantly signed up for visiting instructor Saskia Rushkin's survey course on ecosystems theory. I loved it. Her holistic approach to the Reconstruction enchanted me, as did Saskia herself. For a while there, I even had a bit of a crush on her. Although she was a high level UniTech administrator, she always made time to see me, even after the class ended. When I graduated, she found me a job in one of the many labs she administered.

I don't know when our discussions about astronomy started. They seemed to grow naturally out of our many talks about global systems and earth-sun interactions. In any event, I loved them. Planets, stars, galaxies—it was all so wondrous. Far from drawing me away from my work, however, my love of astronomy made me doubly committed to atmospheric recovery. I was willing to work very hard for the time when the air was clear enough that I could see the stars from the New cities. It might not happen while I was alive, but that didn't matter. Then, one day, Saskia had told me about this fairyland called La Vista, where it was still possible to see the stars and there were scopes to bring them even closer.

Finally, I shook my head and lifted the cup to drain it. As I swallowed, I saw a sweaty and dusty Rubie standing by the door, looking at us.

"Hi," I smiled. "How's it going?"

Rubie said nothing.

"Hey, Rubie," Patrique said, "join us for lunch?"

"I've got to take a bath," Rubie muttered as she brushed by us and into the showers.

I turned in my chair to watch her leave, then faced Patrique again. "She likes me? Who are you kidding?"

Patrique shrugged his shoulders and got up to pour more tea. I shook my head, puzzled. Last night, I had started to think that Rubie liked me, too. Then she'd become so hostile again. Was she still angry from that? Then I wondered if she'd just overheard something that offended her. But there was nothing to overhear, except some babble about Cass and Saskia. *Saskia.* That made me stop for a moment. She was the common factor. Was it possible that the mere mention of her name was enough to work Rubie into a tizzy?

★

I walked out of the cantina and stood in the hall for a moment, wondering what to do. Upstairs or downstairs? I could go to my room and try to rest in preparation for the coming night, but Rubie was up there somewhere. The possibility of running into her did not thrill me. Even if I didn't actually see her, it would be difficult to relax knowing that she was nearby—her hostility was almost palpable. Yes, downstairs was definitely preferable.

I slid the door closed behind me and stood still for a few moments, luxuriating in the warm, rich air of the greenhouse. It was such a pleasant change from the sharp air outside. The light was bright and comforting. As I started strolling down the aisles, stopping now and then to look more closely at the plants, I realized it was almost all food and herbs. Down at one end, though, I saw that someone had taken the trouble to plant a small but colorful bed of flowers. I had to stop there.

Cass loved flowers. She was, in fact, a landscape architect. Her job was to design and implement the many parks and gardens under the

New city domes. UniTech insisted that parks be functional—full of plants that generated lots of oxygen or food—but Cass insured that they were also beautiful. She delighted in shapes and color. Every place she worked on exploded into flowers and berries and graceful trees. It was her gift.

Saskia had never liked Cass. Cass was too light, too beautiful, too frivolous. Technology, to Cass, meant convenience. Convenience—not progress, not passion. She was in love with pleasure. With her, there was always time for pancake breakfasts and sunset walks (not that we had real sunsets, of course, but every night the city dome would swirl with chaotic colors before dimming to night-standard lighting). At night, she'd whisper silly, fantastic stories to me before we fell asleep. One big distraction—that's how Saskia described her—but I couldn't let her go. My relationship with Cass was the only time I ever persistently disregarded Saskia's wishes. I didn't really have a choice: waking up to Cass was like waking up to sunshine. How can you turn your back on the sun?

I used to wonder why Cass stayed with me as long as she did. Me, as solid and predictable as a slab of granite. I think maybe that's why she stuck around. She trusted me. She loved me, too, I knew that, but she loved a lot of people. I was the one she trusted.

I turned away from the flowers. Trust hadn't been enough to keep her. In fact, I suspect that trust was as much of a reason to go. Good, old, dependable, trustworthy Quincy—always there when you need her. Not much excitement in that, is there? No, I hadn't kept her. I wasn't enough.

I walked from the flower beds at a brisk pace, suddenly anxious to be as far from there as possible.

★

Back in the hallway, I was confronted with the same dilemma as before: where to go and what to do? Upstairs was still out, and now so was downstairs. It was too early for any of the astronomers to be stirring. The only people likely to be awake were Patrique and Rubie, and I'd had about all I could take of those two for the time being. Just then, I caught sight of the library across the hall. Browsing through the archives for an hour or two sounded like a fine idea.

The first thing I noticed was that there were real books. I pulled one off the shelf and gingerly opened it. It was paper. Good paper. Real paper books hadn't been made in my lifetime, not since the beginning of the Reconstruction.

The Third Cat had been going on for hundreds of years. It did not refer to a single event, but rather a whole series of occurrences—the wholesale destruction of the environment. Anything that poisoned the air, land, or water fell into the category of the Third: deforestation, oil spills, toxic dumping, ozone holes. One of UniTech's first actions in the Reconstruction was to take over the logging industry and shut it down. This meant no new paper. What existed at the time of UniTech's takeover was endlessly recycled. The only paper I had ever seen had been rough, gray, and almost unreadable.

But this book had fine, fine pages. Aside from being a little yellow with age, the paper was seemingly flawless. Smooth and glorious to the touch. The ink didn't run or smear. The letters were perfect, black and legible. I got out another book. They were all the same. The library was a treasure. There were even star maps in a case by the wall.

Soon my eyes began to ache, and I reluctantly put the books away. If I was going to do any serious reading, I would have to get behind a terminal. Electronics had been UniTech's alternative to paper. Inch for inch, computer memory held billions of times as much information as paper. And computer files could be created, exchanged, and read without felling a single tree. I had learned to read from a screen and write on a keyboard. The old books with the glaring white paper and stark black letters were just too hard on my eyes. I powered up one of the many consoles in the room and started browsing through the on-line library.

Out of curiosity, I used the keyword *astronomy* to search for items. Such a search would have yielded one or two titles at most back home. While I expected there to be more than that on the observatory's computer, I was shocked to see that there were over ten thousand works under that category stored in memory. I stared at the screen, disbelieving. I did the search again. Same result. I brought up the list and started reading the titles and abstracts. They were all about astronomy—books, journals, scientific papers, and data sets. Many of them dated way before the Cats.

I had read over a hundred titles when Theresa, a small, dark woman with a lively smile, poked her head in the room.

"Quincy? Didn't you hear the dinner bell?"

I looked up, disoriented.

"Huh? Oh, no. I was reading."

Theresa grinned at me.

"It's pretty amazing, isn't it? All that information."

"How am I ever going to read it all?" I asked in despair.

Theresa laughed.

"You can't. That's the best part. I haven't even made a dent in the library. Usually, I pick one topic for each visit, something reasonably specific, like R Lyrae stars, and focus on that."

I shook my head, feeling overwhelmed.

"Come on," Theresa said. "Let's go eat dinner. You'll feel better. The universe isn't going anywhere."

I marked my place in the list and got up. My backside was numb from sitting for so long.

After dinner, I got up and made an announcement.

"I thought that I'd do Saskia's ashes tomorrow at sunset. If anyone would like to join me, say a few words or whatever, please come."

Rubie was absent from the table. Off on an overnight trip, someone had said. I would have made the announcement regardless of her presence, but it made it easier not to have to worry about her unpredictable hostility.

"Where were you planning to do it?" Martine asked gently.

"I hadn't really thought about it. Maybe at the summit."

"How about at the top of the NTS?" Martine suggested. "That's at the summit, and there's a walkway around the outside of the dome. Enough room for anyone who wants to come."

"Fine," I said.

"We can meet here after dinner and walk up together," Martine said. "It's a long way to go alone."

Having carried the ashes all the way from New Seattle, I did not think that a kilometer or two to the NTS was so long. But Martine was kind to have thought of that. And it was fitting that it would be at a scope, the biggest scope in the world. Yes, Saskia would have liked that. There was something oddly hopeful in that gesture.

After checking the duty roster for my assignment, I found Jin-Li and headed off to the greenhouse. There was routine maintenance to be done—changing light bulbs, unclogging hoses, and checking on the experimental growing plots. It was pleasant to work with my hands. Jin-Li's constant stream of cheerful talk kept away the gloomy spirits the greenhouse had aroused in me earlier that day. Nevertheless, I stayed as far from the flowers as possible.

When it was dark, I toured the operating domes, visiting with the observers and talking about their projects. I learned how they worked and what they were looking for. I wound up in front of Martine's dome after midnight.

"Am I bothering you?" I asked.

"Hardly, my dear. It's good to see you. I'm afraid that this gets a little tedious when you're by yourself for hours."

I watched her work for a moment before taking a seat.

"Do you know what Saskia was working on?" I asked.

"She used to work in this dome, as a matter of fact," Martine replied, "but I don't think she did any actual observing in the last ten years or so."

"No observing?" I asked, uncomprehending.

What else was there to do up here?

"No. She was far more interested in doing real astronomy."

Now I was confused. I thought observing and astronomy were the same things.

"What do you mean? You're doing astronomy."

Martine chuckled.

"You think so? Look here. I flip this toggle, punch in this number, wait for focus, flip this toggle, record that number. There. Astronomy is about ideas—understanding data, coming up with theories. This here is just legwork. I probably do more astronomy when I'm lying in bed thinking about my results than I do when I'm in the dome."

I stood up and walked to the other side of the control room. This was a little hard to swallow.

"Don't get me wrong, Quincy. This is an important pilgrimage for all of us. La Vista is a shrine for die-hard astronomers like myself. But you can't let the romance of the place fool you and get so hung up on the rituals that you forget the spirit of the endeavor."

It was a ringing injunction from an otherwise mild-mannered woman. I would not have expected it from her. I walked back over to where Martine was sitting. The harsh light from the control panel reflected off her features, showing that kind face set in unnaturally hard lines.

"You know, you almost sounded like Saskia just then," I said. Saskia had been a tough woman.

Martine chuckled, and the hardness disappeared from her features as the smile wrinkles returned to their usual places.

"Well, I guess that's true," Martine replied. "Saskia said almost those exact same words to me years ago. The first several years that I was here, I'd just stake out a scope and observe nonstop. Then I'd store the data somewhere and never look at it again. I thought I was an astronomer. She set me straight, all right. Now I take the time to think about what I've seen and compare it to what other people see. That's astronomy."

I had to smile. Saskia had taken me to task on more than one occasion for presuming to know too much. It was a humbling experience, but one that I was grateful for. Although Saskia had been a hard taskmaster, education, not humiliation, was her goal.

"If you really want to know what Saskia did, go to the library. She spent most of her time there in the last few years, salvaging pre-Cat data and cataloging the stuff we've done since. It's a remarkable collection. I don't know how she got her hands on some of that stuff."

"Do you have a terminal here?" I asked.

This way I could be in a dome and study Saskia's work at the same time. I was a little disappointed that my mentor had chosen to be a librarian instead of an observer, but if Saskia had been working on it, it must have been important. She had not been a woman to waste her time.

"Right over there," Martine said, pointing it out.

I sat down and logged on to the library computer. Thinking back to Theresa's advice, I decided to limit my inquiry to one topic: black holes. Whether we were deriving mathematical proofs or kicking around philosophical pictures of space-time, Saskia and I had never tired of talking about those mysterious objects. I began to skim the list of papers. To my surprise, I saw Saskia's name in the list of authors. It was dated two years ago. I keyed up that article and began to read.

Saskia had not, of course, presented any original data. The NTS had been the only instrument capable of collecting accurate enough information. But what Saskia had done, I realized as I read the article, was nothing short of brilliant. She had gone back to the original NTS studies and culled the data from several different experiments. By merging the data from the various studies and analyzing it with new techniques, she'd managed to come up with several radical and interesting conclusions. Completely original ideas from material that was decades old. I read with a sense of growing awe.

"Hey, Quincy," Martine called, "I'm making tea. You want some?"

"Martine," I said, "come here. Look at this. It's unbelievable."

"What is it?" Martine asked, walking over to the console, blowing at her mug to cool the tea.

"Saskia was not just doing library work. Read this."

I pulled the mildly protesting Martine into the chair.

"Read. I'll go watch the scope and feed in the numbers."

"You feel comfortable with that?"

"Toggle, enter, toggle, wait, record," I recited with a wink.

Martine snorted and shook her head.

"Cheeky thing," she said, unsuccessfully trying to hide a grin. "Holler if you run into problems."

I sat down at the controls. I had a quick rush of adrenaline, but after the first few stars, the procedure seemed completely mundane and I settled easily into the routine.

A long, low whistle from Martine broke the silence in the dome.

"Now that is good science," she said, polishing off her cup of tea as she stood up. "Really exciting stuff."

I glowed with the praise for my mentor.

"I wonder if she did others," I mused.

"Well, get over here and look," Martine said. "Let me have my chair back so I can go back to my boring old stars."

I traded places with her and got to work. There were over two dozen of Saskia's papers in the library, covering virtually every astronomical phenomenon that had ever been studied at La Vista. I started to read them, updating Martine as I discovered each new one.

"This is weird," I said, as I finished reading one of the papers.

"What's weird?" Martine asked, getting up from her chair and stretching.

"The bibliography in this paper. It's incomplete. Saskia makes reference to sources that she doesn't list."

"Well, that doesn't sound like Saskia," Martine said, coming to stand beside me.

"No, it doesn't, does it? She was always so meticulous about that sort of thing. Look here. There's a blank spot where the reference to Gorman's work should be."

"Like it's been erased."

"Yeah."

"Hmm. Probably just a glitch in the transfer system. This terminal is not always reliable. Anyway, it's almost light out. Time to close the dome and go to sleep. Worry about it tomorrow."

I hadn't realized how much time had passed while I was reading the papers. I was very tired. The excitement of discovering Saskia's work had made me forget my exhaustion. I logged off, stretched, and followed Martine outside. It looked like it was going to be a glorious sunrise, but I was too sleepy to stay up and watch.

3

I woke in the early afternoon and tried to go back to sleep. I wanted to be alert when it was time to observe, but my body stubbornly refused to cooperate. I was wide awake. Frustrated, I got out of bed.

Feeling the urge to talk to somebody, I walked up to the solarscope, but Patrique was nowhere to be found. The mirror was covered, and the tracking motor was silent. I looked up. The sky was lined with clouds. Not observing weather at all. I hoped it would clear up by dark.

I continued walking and was soon beyond the domes. There was little danger of getting lost. The NTS dome was visible from miles away, and there was no vegetation to obscure the view, just rocks, sand, and scrub. I picked my way along the rock ridge, aiming to walk to the end and sit.

To the east, I could see the peaks of the Andes. At three thousand meters, La Vista was practically still in the foothills of that great mountain range. My eyes grew accustomed to the subtle colors of the desert as I walked, and I began to realize that I was in a very beautiful place. The bands of red and gold rolling through the hills were dusted with green, no doubt due to the recent rain. Looking closely at the damp ground, I saw tiny purple flowers. I straightened, my head cocked, listening for an unusual sound. There was nothing. That was the unusual sound. Silence, total and absolute. There were no birds, no animals, none of the sounds of the New cities—no hum of generators, no purr of air purifiers. Then the wind whistled past my ear, breaking the spell. I continued walking.

I spotted some unnaturally colorful object ahead of me, just before the ridge came to an abrupt end. As I got closer, I realized it was a piece of nylon webbing looped around a boulder. I edged toward the cliff, trying to determine how high and steep it was. I got down on my stomach and crawled until I could see over the edge. A pair of bright green eyes looked up at me. It was Rubie, clinging to the side of the cliff less than two meters below me.

"Uh, hi," I said, flustered.

Rubie blinked.

"I was just going for a walk," I continued hurriedly, "and I wanted to find out what the neon strap was."

"Well," Rubie said slowly, "at the moment it's keeping me from plunging to the ground, so please don't touch it."

"Oh, no," I said, wiggling backward a meter or so to show that I had no intention of so much as breathing on the thing.

"Patrique is at the bottom belaying me. There's a trail off to your right if you want to join him. I'll be down in a few minutes."

Rubie sounded reasonably pleasant, so I decided to check it out. Whatever caused Rubie's foul moods, she seemed to recover from them quickly. I located the trail without difficulty and began winding my way down. Rubie beat me to the bottom. She and Patrique were surrounded by ropes and other climbing gear I couldn't identify.

"Insomnia?" Patrique asked with a grin when he saw me.

"You got it," I said. "What are you two doing?"

"Rubie's teaching me to climb," he replied. "It consoles me when the weather's bad and I can't do my work."

"You think it'll clear up by tonight?"

"Ask Rubie. She's the weather expert."

Rubie laughed.

"Still smarting from that hailstorm, aren't you, Patrique?"

Patrique gave her a mock growl, which made her laugh more.

"Patrique insisted on going climbing one afternoon," she explained to me. "I told him it would hail, but he didn't believe me."

"The sky was clear!" Patrique interjected.

"Of course, it started to hail," Rubie continued. "Patrique hadn't brought any warm clothes. I lent him one of my sweaters so he wouldn't freeze to death."

"The mirror on my solarscope was pitted from the hail, too. What a mess."

"Needless to say, Patrique no longer ignores my weather forecasts."

I watched this little interchange with amusement. Rubie needled playfully, and Patrique hammed up the chagrin.

"So what's your forecast for tonight?" I asked Rubie.

"Increasing cold and cloudiness," she replied promptly. "Sorry."

Rubie was double-checking Patrique's equipment. They were tied on to opposite ends of the rope that was attached to the rock high above.

"You're on belay," Rubie said to Patrique.

"See you in a bit," Patrique replied.

He approached the rock face and tentatively reached for handholds. Rubie settled herself not far from me, taking up the slack as Patrique climbed and occasionally calling out instructions.

"Do you climb?" Rubie asked after a while.

"No, but I've seen people doing it at the rec center," I said, pleased that Rubie was going to talk to me. I told myself I shouldn't be pleased, that polite conversation was only to be expected, but nevertheless I was pleased. "It looked like fun, but there are other things I'd rather do. I didn't know people climbed outside."

Rubie laughed, and I let myself relax a little. She had a nice laugh.

"That's the only way people climbed for a long time. Of course, that was pre-Cat. This is one of the last areas left that's nontoxic and open to people. Hardly anyone is willing to make the trip up here, so the area is pretty much untouched."

A noise from above caused Rubie to spring into action, jerking the rope she was holding down and to the side. The rope went taut. I looked up. It took me a moment to realize that Patrique had slipped.

"You're okay," Rubie called up to him. "Just hang there for a minute and rest on the rope."

Patrique resumed climbing, and we continued our conversation. We talked quite amiably about climbing, about music, about friends. When my stomach loudly reminded me that I hadn't eaten anything, Rubie insisted I share some of the food she had brought with her. She was charming in her own way. I studied her clear, strong profile. She looked satisfied. When she talked about climbing, her eyes were almost glassy with pleasure. Despite my better judgment, I was really starting to like her.

We walked back to the hotel together. There were a few hours before dinner, so I went to the library, still smiling. It had been a nice afternoon. I pulled up Saskia's papers on the computer and started reading again.

I was on the second paper when I noticed the problem. Every couple of pages, a sentence was scrambled, the words mixed up so that I had to stop for a minute or two to sort out the meaning. It happened often enough for it to be a nuisance. I finished the paper and powered down the terminal. It was time for dinner. I thought back to the incomplete bibliography I'd seen last night and wondered if the two things were connected. It seemed unlikely. But perhaps there was something wrong with the storage unit these papers were on. Hopefully, there were back-ups. I resolved to talk to Patrique about it later that evening.

The dining room seemed strangely subdued when I walked in. Then I remembered that tonight was the night we were going to scatter Saskia's ashes. I'd been so preoccupied all afternoon that I hadn't dwelled on it at all. My appetite diminished appreciably at the thought, and I only picked at my food. When I got up after dinner, a hush fell around the room.

"I'm going to get the ashes," I said, without meeting anyone's eyes. "If you want to come with me, meet me back here in ten minutes or so."

I went to my room and took the container from the closet where I had left it. I sat for a few minutes, just looking at it, then put on my parka and went back to the dining room.

There were about a dozen people waiting for me. Patrique, Martine, Jin-Li, Theresa, and others. They stood up without saying a word and followed me out the door. I started up the road toward the NTS. I saw Rubie sitting on a boulder beyond the road, watching the darkening hills. I wondered briefly what she was thinking. As the group approached her, Rubie turned and scrambled down with considerable agility. To my surprise, she came toward us. For a brief moment I feared that she was going to disrupt the ceremony, but she simply fell into step behind me.

There was a stairway on the outside of the NTS, rising fifteen meters off the ground as it wound around the column. The stairs ended where the straight walls of the column began to curve inward to make the dome. I walked around the catwalk until I was facing west. On this side, the earth dropped away from the dome, almost thirty-five meters straight down. The sun was getting redder and redder as it sunk toward the horizon. The wispy clouds glowed orange and purple.

I stood there, holding the urn, not sure what to do. I felt oddly detached from the moment, as if it were all only a dream—Saskia's death, La Vista, the stars. There were no tears in my eyes, no tension in my throat. I felt a touch on my arm and turned slightly.

It was Rubie. I tensed immediately, wondering what she would do. I half expected the woman to rip the urn from my arms and fling it over the side, or spit on the ashes. But all Rubie did was gently remove the lid from the container. I held my breath as Rubie reached inside and gathered a small handful of ashes.

Rubie leaned on the railing, her fist on her chest, her head down. When she looked up, the burning light of the sunset ran in the streams of tears on her face. Her lips were moving, but I heard no sound. Rubie leaned out further, and for one insane moment, I thought she was going to jump. Instead, she extended her arm and slowly opened her fist. The wind caught the ashes as they sifted through her fingers.

Rubie backed away. One by one the others approached me and took a pinch out of the container. Some said a few words before they scattered the ashes, but mostly there was silence. I stood with my eyes closed, my thoughts eight months in the past.

Cass up and left, just like that. She packed her things while I was at work and disappeared. No note, no explanation, nothing. There was no forwarding address. She was simply gone. I didn't think people did things like that, removed themselves from your life with one clean swoop. It was like an amputation that nobody bothered to bandage up. Several days later, I stumbled into the lab out of mindless habit. I was completely numb. Saskia found me like that, just sitting there, unable even to think. I gave her the explanation she demanded. Saskia had disapproved of the relationship from the start, and she disapproved of emotional outbursts in general, so I made my explanation as light and detached as possible. I even tried to make a joke about it. To my surprise, Saskia murmured a brief consolation and that was it. No admonition to return to work, no I told you so, no condemnation of Cass. Just a sympathetic word, then she left me in peace.

Saskia returned several hours later with some news. I stared at her, open-mouthed, as she recited Cass's present whereabouts, her new job prospects, and even the name of her new lover. The news in itself was hard to process, but I was equally stunned that Saskia had gone to the trouble of finding it out. She had to have pulled some serious strings to obtain that information so quickly.

"I can get her back," Saskia stated flatly, while I was still digesting the news.

I just stared at her, not understanding.

"I can get her back," she said again, looking around to make sure no one could hear her. "Just say the word. I have some influence. I'll have her back here on a priority transfer by the first of next week. Or I can see to it that she won't find work out there. Hell, I can close the North Atlantic Station if I have to."

If I had ever doubted that Saskia loved me, here was undeniable proof she did. I knew she could and would do what she promised, even though it meant bringing a woman she detested back into my life. That was devotion. It was not, however, an offer I could accept. Cass had left of her own free will. I wasn't going to have her dragged back just because my heart was broken. Still, it was a huge consolation to know that Saskia loved me enough to offer.

That memory faded and another welled up.

I was twenty-one. My designs for the New Tucson filter project had caught the eye of the Regional Science Committee, and I'd been called up to report. It became clear almost immediately that while the committee wanted my designs, they did not want me. I was too young and inexperienced to head such an important project, they claimed. Saskia was sitting in on the meeting, the cool and impartial science administrator. I kept hoping she would defend me, but she was quiet. During a break, I escaped to the bathroom to snivel over my loss and her defection. Saskia followed me. I expected an apology, or at least an explanation, but I got neither.

"Quincy Alexander," she roared. "I have never, until this moment, believed that your age or experience disqualified you from any project. But now I have to wonder. That project was yours, and you let them take it away from you without a fight. Are you a woman or a girl?"

That little speech dried my tears faster than the hot air blow-dryer. I marched back into the room and began to fight. Saskia refused to look at me, but I kept at it until everyone's patience was worn thin. I couldn't bear to have Saskia think of me as a feckless girl. Finally, the committee appealed to her to talk some sense into me. I sank back into my chair, defeated. When she stood up, I knew she was going to repeat the speech she *had given me in the bathroom.*

"Dr. Alexander," she said, "is simply the finest design engineer I have ever had the privilege of having under my administration. There is no person better suited to head this project. Her age is simply not an issue."

The debate was over. Later, I thanked her for changing her mind about me and giving me another chance.

"I never changed my mind, Quincy," she replied. "I always believed you were the one for the job. I just wanted you to fight for yourself. You doubt your ability unnecessarily. You're far more clever than I was at your age. You'll go far."

And she gave me a hug, the first and only hug I ever got from her. Actually, it was little more than a swift, double-handed pat on the back. It was terribly awkward—full of the stiff rigidity of a straight woman trying to express her affection for a lesbian without actually touching bodies—but that hug burned into me a profound conviction of my worth and her perfection. I was marked as hers from that moment on.

I opened my eyes and was back at La Vista. All of the others had passed by, and only a tiny pile of ashes remained. I lifted the container high. I thought I should say something. This was the woman who had first been my idol, then my teacher, then my friend. I could almost feel those iron hands of hers pressed into my back like hot brands.

"Good-bye," I whispered, and there was nothing else to say.

I tilted the container, and the ashes ran out in a fine, silver stream. There were no tears left inside of me, only the dull empty ache of loneliness. I shook the urn once, then put it down.

I don't know who carried it back. I walked in a fog to the hotel and went straight to the showers. I sat down in one of the stalls, turning the water up as hot as I could stand it.

When I finally emerged, I heard people talking and laughing in the common room. I didn't feel like being around a crowd. On the other hand, I was sure to get deathly depressed if I was all alone. I considered going to the domes instead. During dinner, Francoise had invited me to take over her project when she left. Maybe it would be a good time to talk about the work. I certainly felt the need to be distracted.

I was ten steps outside the hotel when the door closed behind me.

I stopped abruptly, waiting for my eyes to adjust to the darkness. Nothing happened. I turned around, but the hotel was completely light tight, and I could not make it out in the darkness. I looked up for the faint, reassuring light of the stars. There was nothing but blackness. Clouds, I told myself, it's just cloudy. But the total absence of light was disorienting, and I felt a flicker of panic. I fumbled for my flashlight and then realized I had left it in my room. The urge to scream was growing.

"Quincy."

I spun in the direction of the voice. It was Patrique. He had just come out of the hotel. The small flashlight in his hand seemed incredibly bright. I focused on the light, feeling very relieved.

"Are you okay?" he asked.

"I forgot my light," I replied in a small voice, beginning to feel foolish.

"That can be scary," said another voice.

I could just make out the shape of a second person standing next to Patrique. Rubie, of course. Patrique's constant companion these days. I didn't allow myself to dwell on it. I explained to them that I'd been on my way to see Francoise in her dome.

"It's too cloudy," Patrique said. "Nobody is observing tonight. They're all in the common room. I think they were going to watch a video."

"Did you want to see the video? I think it's a comedy," Rubie offered.

"Oh, no," I said. "I don't really feel like being around a lot of people."

"It's been kind of a rough night," Patrique said sympathetically.

"Would you like to join us for a drink, then? We were going to open a bottle," said Rubie.

"Yes," Patrique said. "Join us."

Both of them were warm and sincere, and it sounded like a lot more fun than moping alone in my room. I gratefully agreed. Rubie and Patrique walked on either side of me, lighting my path with their flashlights.

"Where are we going?" I asked, quickly realizing that we were not returning to the hotel.

"My quarters are separate from the main building," Patrique explained. "There are actually several barracks around here, but since there are so few of us, we usually only use the ones at the hotel. I like a little extra privacy, though."

Patrique's room was large and well-lighted. There were pictures on the wall as well as other decorative touches that suggested the room had been lived in for a long time. I took one of the chairs. Patrique pulled a wooden box from the closet and pried open the lid. Almost reverently, he lifted out a bottle, brushing off the straw packing.

"What is it?" I asked.

"Pisco!"

It was not a word I recognized. I assumed it was alcoholic.

"A grape brandy," Rubie explained, sensing my confusion. "Before the Cats, it was Chile's national beverage."

"And this is a particularly fine bottle," Patrique added.

"Where'd you get it?"

"There's a huge stash in one of the rooms down here," Patrique explained. "Back when La Vista was operational, alcohol was officially forbidden. Didn't want to distract the astronomers from the serious business of observing, I guess. Apparently, though, the astronomers didn't agree with the policy. This was probably smuggled in here over seventy years ago."

He poured a glass and motioned for me to try it. I sipped tentatively. It was warm and smooth, sliding down my throat like honey.

"Wow," I murmured appreciatively.

Patrique and Rubie both laughed and then poured some for themselves. Patrique sat in the other chair and Rubie settled herself on the bed. We drank in comfortable silence for a while.

"All the comforts of home," I mused. "And then some. But I guess this is your home, Patrique. Do you ever think about going back?"

"Not unless UniTech plans on pardoning me."

I just stared at him. He took another swallow and explained.

"Three years ago, I was caught doing illegal research on the UniTech computer Network. I was working on my own time, of course, but forbidden topics are forbidden no matter when you work on them."

"What were you doing?"

"Looking at the deep internal structure of the sun. It was actually quite a big field before the Cats. Tons of data was collected that never got analyzed, so I fed it through the computers and started studying it. I just wanted to see what the sun looked like inside. That was my crime. I wouldn't have gone to jail, not on a first offense, but I would never have been allowed near a computer again. A permanent demotion. It would have driven me out of my mind."

"All for the heinous crime of astronomy," I said, shaking my head.

"Yes. Since it's not immediately useful to the Reconstruction, it must be evil science."

"Now, Patrique," Rubie started, "UniTech has done a lot of good."

"I know that. I'm not saying they haven't. God knows, they probably saved the planet. I'm just...mourning my loss."

"So you came here to lead your life of crime in peace," I said.

"Yes. And for the most part, I have no regrets. I go back every year or so to say hello to friends, but everything else I could want is here."

"A man of few needs," I remarked.

"I admire you, Patrique," Rubie added. "Not being an astronomer myself, I don't understand the allure."

"An acquired taste," Patrique said, draining his cup with a flourish.

He reached out to refill our glasses. Rubie just snorted.

We turned to other subjects, talking our way through half the bottle. I was just starting to feel alert when I noticed that my companions were yawning. They were not used to staying up all night. I wondered if I should ask to borrow one of their flashlights so I could get back to the hotel. Perhaps they were waiting for me to leave. What if, God forbid, Rubie and Patrique were lovers? Rubie didn't strike me as that type of woman, but it wasn't completely implausible.

To my pleased surprise, when I mentioned leaving, Rubie stood up and said she would accompany me. We said goodnight to Patrique and stepped outside. It was still cloudy. Moreover, the temperature had dropped several degrees since we went inside.

"You were right about the weather," I remarked.

"Always am," she replied smugly. "Brrr."

"Well, if you're so weather smart, where's your parka?" I asked.

"I left it in my room. Patrique waylaid me in the common room, and I forgot to go back for it. Come on, let's jog. That'll keep us warm."

She grabbed me by the elbow and started to run. I laughed as I struggled to keep up. The alcohol in my stomach made me feel silly and flushed. It also made it difficult for me to walk in a straight line, much less run. I leaned against Rubie for support.

"What are you doing now?" Rubie asked as we walked inside.

"I need to stay awake and keep on my schedule," I said. "I'll go talk to Francoise, maybe, or do some reading if I can't find her."

"Well, it's past my bedtime," Rubie said, starting up the stairs toward the living quarters.

Seeing as how Rubie was still holding on to my arm, I seemed obliged to follow her. We stopped outside her door. Rubie let go of my arm.

"Thanks for inviting me to have a drink," I said, missing the pressure of Rubie's hand on my arm.

"You looked like you needed it," Rubie said, leaning up against the wall next to me.

Rubie's hand brushed mine. I felt giddy. Damn, but Rubie was attractive when she was being friendly. I knew I was grinning foolishly, but I couldn't help it. I tried to remember how much I'd had to drink.

"You're right," I said. "I feel much better than I did a few hours ago. And I really enjoyed hanging out with you two. It cheered me up."

"A pleasure," Rubie replied softly.

Oh God, I thought, as I looked at her. Rubie's green eyes seared right through me, down my spine and into my crotch. Again her hand brushed mine, light and electric.

A door opened down the hall. I started slightly. Francoise came out of her quarters and waved to us.

"Hey, Quincy," she called. "Are you busy? Want to go over the project now?"

"Uh, sure," I replied. "I'll meet you in the reading room in a minute."

Francoise disappeared up the stairs. I turned back to Rubie. One part of me ached to know what would have happened if Francoise had not appeared when she did. But another part of me was relieved. I had almost been delirious there for a moment. It had happened frighteningly fast. I needed time to think.

"Well, goodnight," I said awkwardly.

"Goodnight, Quincy," Rubie said quietly as she retreated into her room and shut the door.

So much for Patrique and Rubie being lovers, I thought.

I went and made myself some tea before joining Francoise. I even managed to stay reasonably focused for most of the discussion. Afterward, I disappeared into the library to read. I called up one of Saskia's papers, but despite the interesting topic, I couldn't manage to concentrate on it. I was very tired and still slightly drunk. The text seemed to waver on the page, and the writing felt remarkably garbled. I logged off. It was still an hour before dawn, but I went to bed anyway.

4

Finally, my body was getting used to the observing schedule. I slept well into the afternoon. By the time I'd gotten dressed and straightened my room, I was almost late for dinner. I took the stairs two at a time.

I had to smile when I saw that there was an empty seat next to Rubie. I filled my plate and sat down. I chatted with Jin-Li who was on my other side, but the hairs on my right arm were keenly attuned to Rubie's every movement. I told myself to stop acting like a girl. I was a scientist—I'd come here to do astronomy. This was silliness. Still, the giddiness in my stomach made it hard for me to eat much.

"Guess what?" Theresa said, as she came up behind me and put her hands on my shoulders.

The announcements were finished, and people were starting to disperse to do their various chores. I was actually glad of Theresa's appearance. I'd been struggling to think of something to say to Rubie, and the silence had been getting awkward.

"What? Oh, that feels wonderful," I said.

Theresa had started to rub my shoulders, digging her thumbs into the place where I store all my anxiety. It felt good to consign it to someone else's hands.

"You and I," Theresa said, "have pulled the primo duty assignment."

"And what's that? Oh, yes, right there."

Theresa had found a knot in my back. I couldn't remember the last time someone had massaged my shoulders.

"We get to clean the bathrooms!"

Rubie, who turned in her chair to watch us, laughed at the expression on my face.

"Well, I'll leave you to it," Rubie said, getting up. She gave us both a gentle slap on the back. "Catch you later."

Theresa and I took the cleaning supplies out of the closet and headed for the bathroom. We decided to do the toilets first and get the worst part over with.

"I'll start the showers while you do the sinks," Theresa said, when we emerged from the stalls.

I fell to work. I scrubbed with single-minded intensity, anxious to get this done and see what the rest of the evening held.

"Work that sponge," came a breathy encouragement in my ear.

I straightened and saw Rubie standing next to me.

"Hi," I said, smiling. Just the person I wanted to see.

"I don't think I've ever seen a shine like this," Rubie continued, wetting her toothbrush under a nearby faucet. "Carla would probably make this your permanent assignment if you asked her."

I watched as Rubie spread thick white paste onto her brush. I shook my head slightly and turned back to my sink.

"No, no," I said lightly. "I wouldn't want to deprive anyone else of the pleasure."

"Looks like it'll be a clear night," Rubie said when she was finished brushing her teeth. She hitched herself up on the counter and pulled out the floss. "You'll be observing with Francoise?"

"Yep," I said, moving on to the next sink. "I'm going to finish up her project when she's gone. With all the bad weather, she hasn't gotten to do everything she wanted. It'll be good experience for me."

"Maybe I can come up one night and see what you do," Rubie said.

I looked over to where she was splashing her face with water. Considering what I'd seen so far of Rubie's attitude towards astronomy, the request struck me as strange. Still, I wasn't about to turn her down.

"Any time," I said, as casually as I could. "Star talk is one of my favorite things."

"Great," Rubie said, her words muffled by the towel with which she was drying her face. "I'll see you."

"Bye."

I stopped working to watch her leave. I didn't quite know what to make of the woman. Theresa emerged from the showers, and I quickly turned back to the sinks. Theresa started cleaning the mirrors.

"Be careful," Theresa said, after we had worked in silence for a few minutes.

"Of what?" I asked, puzzled. I'd been off in dreamland.

Theresa inclined her head toward the door through which Rubie had recently departed.

"Your heart."

"What do you mean?"

I had finished the last sink. I leaned against the wall and looked at Theresa.

"Rubie is a wonderful person," Theresa said, rubbing at a spot that I couldn't see. "But she's not someone I trust emotionally. She won't be careful with your feelings."

I felt a tiny bit of resentment toward Theresa. Who asked her, anyway?

"It's probably none of my business," Theresa said, as if reading my thoughts, "but you seem like you could get hurt."

I drew in a deep breath. I *was* lonely. Saskia's death had left a huge void in my life. Cranky and demanding as the old woman had been, she had also been like a mother to me. And Cass' defection—well, that had devastated me too. Since she'd left, I had had no interest in dating. I'd worked long hours to avoid socializing. And now, here was Rubie. Moody and unpredictable, it was true. She was, nonetheless, immensely attractive. Those few moments in the hall last night had stirred me in ways I'd forgotten.

"Thanks," I said sincerely. "I'll try to keep it in mind."

I would keep it in mind. Not that it would do any good. Hearts, as I had often observed in myself and in others, rarely responded to reason.

I picked up a towel and started working on the full-length mirror by the door.

"You know, it's funny," I said in an attempt to lighten the mood, "but I thought at first that Rubie had a thing for Patrique."

"Well, she very well might have at some point in the last few weeks," Theresa said, polishing the last corner with an extra-hard swipe. "Rubie does tend to get around."

I looked into Theresa's eyes, surprised by the heaviness I saw there. Suddenly, several little things clicked into place.

"You?" I asked softly.

Theresa nodded unhappily.

"Just briefly," she said. "We spent a lot of time together the first couple of days I was here."

"I'm sorry."

Theresa shrugged.

"It was stupid," she said. "I'm embarrassed that it happened. She's not that great a lover anyway. Kind of detached, you know, like she wasn't all there."

I didn't know, but I nodded just the same. It was costing Theresa a lot to share this with me, and I appreciated her willingness to do so.

"Thanks for telling me."

"Yeah, well. Listen, why don't you go get the broom while I shake the mats?"

"Sure thing," I said, relieved to be off the topic.

When we were done cleaning, I went straight to the dome where Francoise was working. Earlier, I'd been planning to stop by Rubie's room and chat for a few minutes before heading up. But I decided against it. Theresa had given me a lot to think about.

"Think you can handle it by yourself?" Francoise said after we'd been through the procedure several times.

"What are you going to do now?"

"I'm going to take a pill and try to sleep. I need to get back on a normal schedule before I hike down."

"All right, then. Sleep tight."

"You're coming to the party tomorrow night, aren't you?"

"Certainly," I replied.

After Francoise left, I settled down to work. There was more slack time in this project than there had been at Martine's. I would type in commands, wait several minutes, make some adjustments, and wait several more minutes. Naturally, my thoughts began to wander.

Rubie was, of course, in the forefront of my mind. We had sort of started a relationship, but I had real doubts, and not just because of what Theresa said. Rubie was unfathomable at times. I remembered our first meeting out there on the trail. No, it had not been an auspicious beginning, not at all.

I thought back to what it was like in the beginning with Cass. There was really no comparison. She was a friend of one of the guys in my lab. I knew all along that I was falling in love with her, and that she probably barely even noticed me. Surely I wasn't the reason for her frequent visits to the lab. The astonishment I felt when she leaned over the coffee pot to kiss me one afternoon was unrivaled in its intensity. I had never felt that way before, and doubted that I would again.

I'd been so naive when I met Cass—a passion for air filters will keep you innocent for a long time—but she hadn't held it against me. No, in fact, she'd reveled in my naiveté. "It's so refreshing," she used to say. It pleased her to ferret out my pockets of ignorance and to educate me. Her tutorials were, by and large, very pleasant experiences. One of the most memorable lessons was about the sensuality of food. I remembered that before I met Cass, I'd been possessed by the notion that food and sex didn't mix. Cass was astonished at this lack of adventurousness and set out to change it. She had to be devious, though, because there was no way I'd have gone for it if she'd just announced her intentions. She was very devious.

I'd had a bad day at the lab, and I came home fretful and depressed. Cass only took one look at me before throwing me onto the bed, stripping me down, and pounding my muscles into relaxation. I protested when she got up, but she promised to return promptly with my favorite snack, a hot fudge sundae.

She spooned a few bites into my mouth, and I drifted in and out of wakefulness, deliciously fulfilled. After a while, I could feel my bellybutton being filled with a warm, soft liquid. I cracked my eyes to see Cass lapping fudge out of my navel. She spooned up more and made a dribbling track up my chest. Since I had been so opposed to this sort of thing in the past, I couldn't let on that I was enjoying it. I pretended to be asleep.

My pretense was nearly discovered at one point when, having been following the warm track of fudge across my breast, and fully anticipating one last generous drop, I got instead a dollop of ice cream. I just barely kept myself from yelping at the cold. Almost instantly, Cass leaned in to consume the ice cream and warm my hard, chilled nipple in her mouth.

It was a slow, delicious torture. Up and down my body: chocolate, ice cream, tongue. Between my toes, inside my elbows, in my mouth. At one point I weakly protested the mess, and the sorry state the sheets were sure to be in.

"You're supposed to be asleep," Cass replied.

I shut up and lay still. The sweet delight continued. After a while, Cass put her hand on the inside of my thigh, and I spread my legs without a sound. Then the rest of the sundae came pouring down me, spilling warmth and chills through my pubes. I completely forgot about the stickiness and the mess. Everything in the world ceased to exist except for her mouth on my cunt. Her tongue went down one side then up the middle, getting gentler as it rose to the clit, and then down the other side, over and over until I came in a long, long shudder of sweet, hot, cold.

She'd already run a bath, so I was soaking in warm soapy water before the stickiness got unpleasant. Cass was always thinking ahead about things like that. And I couldn't help but come again when she washed me clean. I almost always came when Cass wanted me to. It seemed impossible for me to resist her. I never got enough.

But she'd gotten enough of me.

That thought ended my happy memory, and my distinctly damp underwear immediately began to dry. I fidgeted uncomfortably in my chair. This kind of nostalgia was unproductive. There was no use dreaming of how things used to be, or wishing that they'd been different.

I focused my attention back on the scope. I discovered a way to log on to the library computer from my terminal so that when there was slack time in the observation, I could devote myself to reading Saskia's papers. It was excellent mental discipline. Lost in graphs and theories, I could almost forget that both Cass and Rubie existed.

It was approaching dawn when I knew for sure that something was terribly wrong with the papers. Two out of the four I'd read that night had problems. In one, several diagrams were missing. In the other, every letter *e* had been replaced by an *a*. The whole thing was very weird.

It was getting too light to see the stars, so I closed the dome and turned off the scope. I composed a long note to Patrique about the difficulties I'd run into and posted it to the terminal at the solarscope. He'd see it as soon as he started his scope. I would talk to Carla and Martine later.

Feeling like I'd done all I could for the moment, I logged off and left the scope. I grabbed a bite to eat on my way through the dining room, saying hello to the other astronomers who'd come in at the same time. Then, as I crawled under the covers, I tried to figure out whether I was relieved or disappointed that Rubie had not visited me in the dome that night. I fell asleep without reaching a decision.

★

I went in search of Patrique as soon as I woke up. He was in the library. I could tell by his face that all was not well.

"We definitely have a problem," he said grimly, swiveling around to face me. "Two-thirds of Saskia's files have been corrupted to some degree. Fortunately, the damage is generally slight."

"Back-ups?"

"Those, too."

"Any idea what's wrong?" I asked hopefully.

He shook his head.

"I've been through everything I can think of. The hardware's fine, no trace of physical damage in the memory chips, nothing. Carla and Martine are equally puzzled."

I sighed and took a seat next to his. It was certainly a blow. Saskia's work was dear to me simply because she had done it. Her strong and lively voice came through even the driest of her scientific writings. But these particular papers were brilliant, Saskia's keen mind at its finest. Their loss was nothing short of tragic.

"Don't look so depressed, Quincy," Patrique said encouragingly. "You said the papers were still readable, right? It might take a little work to decipher them, but it's not like they're lost forever or anything."

"Yeah," I shrugged.

It was nice of him to try to cheer me up, but I still felt like bawling. Patrique seemed to sense my mood, because he shut up and left me alone. Whatever anybody said about him, he was still a decent guy. Then it struck me that the only person who'd ever said anything bad about him was Rubie—a woman whose behavior as a lover was, apparently, not above reproach. I pondered that for a while. Finally, I gave up trying to figure anything out about anybody and went to dinner.

It was going to be another foul weather night. That was bad for observing but good for the going-away party. With clouds in the sky, no one felt the need to be racing off to the domes, or to refuse that second glass of home brew. I stopped in the kitchen to help with the preparations and popped some corn. A little salt, a little cheese powder from my pack, and I was ready.

The music was already at a pretty frenetic level by the time I arrived. With all the festivity, I quickly forgot about the papers. Nobody was dancing, so I grabbed Theresa and did a little farewell jig. I was feeling lively. Then I snagged Martine and danced with her a bit, too. Pretty soon, half the room was given over to wild dancing. Francoise and Jin-Li whirled by me, and Patrique did cartwheels. Exhausted but happy, I collapsed into a corner to watch. Someone gave me a cup of beer, which I drank thirstily.

I spotted Rubie over by the food table. She smiled as I approached her.

"You look like you're having a great time," she said.

"Yes! Want to dance?"

"Maybe in a little bit," she said. "What I really want right now is more of this delicious popcorn."

Apparently other people had liked it too because the bowl was empty.

"Let's go make some more, then," I suggested.

As we walked out, I glimpsed Theresa over by the window, looking at us with concern. I waved to her reassuringly and pointed at the bowl. She nodded and looked away. That's when I began to wonder if she was still interested in Rubie. I assumed that Theresa had not been the one to end their affair, and although she didn't seem like the jealous type to me, I began to question her motives in warning me off Rubie. Then I remembered my resolution not to try to understand why people did what they did and I stopped thinking about the matter.

Rubie kept me company while I made the popcorn. I was surprised at how talkative she could be. It was a pleasant change from her dark and silent pose, and I found her sharp wit immensely entertaining.

"Why were you looking so glum when you walked into the party tonight?"

I explained the problem with the computer, omitting, of course, the name of the author of the damaged papers.

"Sounds like you've got a sick computer," Rubie said.

"Sure does, doesn't it?"

"Too bad you can't hook it up to MedCen and engineer a cure, like you did for me," she said, leaning over a little to tap the wrist access of my IMC.

Her hand lingered for just a moment, lightly brushing the inside of my arm. I closed my eyes, feeling the skin burn where she had touched it. It was a decidedly coy seduction, each fleeting touch radiating deeper and deeper into my skin until I could sense the desire in my bones. I'd forgotten what it was like to be weak with need. It had been so long since I'd burned like this. I thought Cass had taken the burning with her when she left.

Thinking of burning reminded me of the popcorn I was tending. I rescued it just in time and put it in the bowl with all the toppings. It occurred to me that I could suggest we take the popcorn back to my room and enjoy it alone, but something held me back. Maybe it was Theresa's warnings. More probably it was because I move slowly, no matter how my clit is jumping. Besides, a slow burn is not entirely unpleasant.

We went back to the party. Someone had turned off the overhead lights. There were small circles of light near the lamps, and candles had been lit all around the room. The dancing continued in one corner, more intense now that the light was low. I deposited the popcorn and got punch for both of us.

"How about that dance?" I asked after a few minutes. I am not terribly good at party talk, and it was difficult to be heard above the din of the music.

"Lead on," Rubie said, putting her glass down.

I began to thread my way through the crowd. Fifty people seemed like a lot when they were all crammed into the same room. I caught Rubie's hand so I wouldn't lose her. She followed very close behind me, and I could feel her breath tickling the hairs on the back of my neck.

Rubie was an enthusiastic dancer once she got started. It was a pleasure to watch her. We were by the wall, behind the other dancers, and I could look at her without being too obvious. I loved to dance and hardly ever felt self-conscious when I was moving. The presence of another free spirit only increased my energy.

The more we danced, the closer we moved together, the slower our motions became. At one point, she rubbed herself on my thigh and I put my arms around her back to support her weight. Her skin was wet and hot under my palms. The delirium of this slow grind was heightened by the fast, driving music and the whirl of dancers around us. I dared to look in her eyes. She smiled.

We stayed like that for quite a while, switching thighs from time to time. It helped that I couldn't see Theresa from where I stood. I was soaring on adrenaline, each near-touch of Rubie's breasts against mine flooding me until I was weak with it. Just when I thought I couldn't stand up on my own anymore, she disengaged herself and led me to the wall behind us. She turned my shoulders so that my back was to her, and pulled me in. I closed my eyes as I felt her breasts sink into my back. She touched my neck and shoulders, harder now, rubbing the tight muscles until I relaxed completely against her.

I opened my eyes a little. It seemed like everyone was dancing in couples. Martine and Carla swept close by us as they made a stately circuit of the dance floor. Nearby, Jin-Li and someone I thought was named Robin were just rocking back and forth. I let one of my hands fall back to rest on Rubie's leg.

The music stopped abruptly, and people fell still.

"Listen, everyone. It's clearing out there," Carla announced. "In about twenty minutes, we're going to have terrific observing."

Some people groaned, some sighed. The music was turned back on, but the dancing did not resume.

"Are you going?" Rubie asked in my ear.

I sighed. I didn't want to, but I really felt that I should. I hadn't come all this way to have a fling; I'd come to study the stars. My body, however, did not appreciate this reasoning. Pulling away from Rubie's embrace was almost painful.

"Yes," I said, turning to face her, "much as I'd rather not. I'm really sorry."

I considered kissing her good-bye. It seemed the natural thing to do, but Rubie had an increasingly distant look in her eyes. I didn't blame her. I would have felt the same way if I'd been abandoned for some crummy old stars.

"Are you going to stay here?" I asked, thinking she might come visit me in the dome later.

Her eyes seemed to be looking at something far away. Slowly, she focused on me.

"Yes," she said coolly. "I'd like to spend some time with Theresa. After all, it is her going away party."

Surprised by Rubie's bristle, I started to apologize again, but she was already halfway across the room. The vibrant intimacy of a few minutes before had evaporated completely. The reference to Theresa especially stung me.

★

I escaped to the dome.

Sitting in the cold control room by myself gave me plenty of time to ponder what had happened that evening. I became more and more upset as I dissected each moment. I knew beyond a shadow of a doubt that Rubie was going to sleep with Theresa that night. It had been in her voice. She was punishing me for leaving. God, I thought, what a despicable thing for her to do.

I considered my options. I could sit here and rot for the rest of the night, or I could go back and make a scene. I could just picture it: storming into the hotel and smashing the door to Rubie's room; tearing Theresa away from Rubie and sending her careening down the stairs. This would, of course, forever endear me to Rubie, who would then cast her half-clad body into my arms and beg me to finish the deed that Theresa had ineptly and clumsily started. I would then pull off her underwear and bury my face in her wet pussy. Yeah, right. I laughed in a grim sort of way. The idea went beyond stupid. If Rubie and Theresa wanted to fuck, that was their business, not mine. Besides, Saskia would have derided me for so much as thinking about abandoning my scope for a woman. *You're at La Vista now, girl. The nights are for stars, not for lovers.* That's what she would have said.

Still, the stars were small solace to me that night. Every time I looked away from the instruments, visions of Rubie filled my head. Rubie with her shirt unbuttoned, Rubie glistening with sweat and honey, Rubie all still and serene. Yet even in my fantasies, I was not the one who touched her, held her, relaxed beside her—it was Theresa. I could not even dream myself into Rubie's bed.

Just when I thought my imaginings couldn't get any more excruciating, they did. The same scenes kept replaying, but this time it wasn't Rubie who lay beyond my reach. It was Cass. Cass in bed with that damned oceanologist whose name I could never remember, wracked by orgasms so intense she almost hit the ceiling.

I knew she didn't love that woman. No, the oceanologist was only an excuse, a way of breaking out of our comfortable domesticity. Someone had to stop the slow suffocation of our relationship, and Cass was the only one with the courage to do it. Oh, I tried everything I could to save us. I did things for her that I never imagined I could do. I put my fingers up her ass, my fist in her vagina. I tied her up and blindfolded her and bought a cabinet full of sex toys. It worked for a while, but never for very long. Just when I felt comfortable enough to come, she pulled back. I was just too safe, too goddamn trustworthy. Cass lived and came on the edge of fear—anonymous sex was the only kind that really turned her on. If it wasn't new and strange, it wasn't sexual. My novelty wore off quickly. She still got me off regularly, and seemed to enjoy doing it, but when I reached for her, she turned away. I'd wake in the night, feel her masturbating next to me, and knew she was not thinking of me when her hand moved on her clit. No, she was thinking of some faceless stranger in a dark corner of the sex rooms in the rec center. I lay there, night after night, drinking in the slow poison of inadequacy.

Suddenly, I was overwhelmed by an immense wave of guilt. I'd never let myself acknowledge it before, but when Cass had left, my feeling of loss had been matched only by my sense of relief. God. Cass had left and I'd been relieved. I hadn't wanted her to leave, had I? I tried to push the thought out of my head, but I couldn't. I'd wanted her to go. Considering how much I loved her, it seemed like a terrible sin.

Finally, I got tired of torturing myself. I was thoroughly demoralized, depressed, and exhausted. I forced myself to stop dwelling on Cass or Rubie, and swore that I would not think about anything with the slightest sexual overtones. I devoted myself to the scope, but punching the codes and commands into the machine made me incredibly weary. I was so physically drained that even lifting my finger was an effort. I just wished the night was over so that I could go to bed, so that I could sleep and forget. As it was, I left the dome earlier than I really should have.

5

I woke feeling as surly as I had the night before. Surlier, in fact, when I remembered that Theresa and I were supposed to cook dinner together. I dressed slowly and kept finding small things to do. Finally, I had no excuse but to head downstairs.

The kitchen was empty except for Martine. Grateful for the temporary reprieve, I sat on a stool and put my head down on the counter.

"Rough night?" Martine asked after a few moments.

I looked up. She was holding out a mug of hot chocolate and motioning for me to take it.

"Thanks," I said, a bit embarrassed by my churlishness.

"Drink it. Chocolate and caffeine—there's no better stimulant."

I sipped for a few minutes, wondering where Theresa was. Dinner would be late if we didn't get started soon.

"Theresa and I switched chores," Martine said, as if reading my thoughts.

"Oh." That was a pleasant surprise. "Well, then I'd better get myself in gear."

Martine was assembling ingredients on the opposite counter. I walked over and started chopping vegetables. Martine turned on some music, and the work went quickly. I liked Martine. Although I knew very little about her, I would have called her a friend.

"How long have you been at La Vista?" I asked.

"Carla and I came up here after we retired from UniTech. It must have been, oh, almost four years ago."

"Before Patrique came?"

"Yes. That's right. He came the year after that."

"Do you miss New Domingo?"

Martine pursed her lips, then shrugged.

"No, not really. I once had a little sister, Leah, who meant the world to me. But she died several years ago. After that, there was nothing left to hold me there."

The lines in Martine's handsome face had deepened at the mention of her sister. I could tell that she still missed her. I murmured sympathetically. At the sound of my voice, Martine roused herself out of her melancholy and shot me a keen look.

"It's probably hard for you to understand, isn't it?" she asked.

"A little," I admitted.

The concept of family was a strange one to me. Womb babies were a relic of pre-Catastrophe days. Constantly surrounded by the toxins and virals of the Cats, a woman's body was no longer enough to protect a fetus. And few people could be spared from the important tasks of the Reconstruction to raise children. I had been born in a UniTech birthing lab and raised in a communal crèche. My parents had dropped in every month or so to visit, and they brought me presents on my birthday. We weren't close friends, but I liked them. I had no knowledge of any siblings.

"Saskia was probably the closest thing I had to family," I said.

Martine said nothing for a while.

"I'm glad to hear it, Quincy," she finally responded, "for your sake and for hers. I never thought of Saskia as being part of anyone's family. I thought the labs were the only home she had. She was the most dedicated science administrator I knew."

The tone of voice in which Martine articulated that last sentence made me wonder if she meant it as a compliment. For the first time, I found myself thinking about the cost of such dedication. Saskia had not had many friends outside of work. Lots of colleagues, lots of students, but few friends. I had been an exception. People just weren't so important to Saskia. Much as I loved and admired her, I wasn't sure that I wanted to imitate her in this respect.

We worked on, chopping and frying. I kept wanting to ask Martine a question, but I wasn't sure how to phrase it without appearing suspicious. Eventually, I just blurted it out.

"Did Theresa say why she wanted to change shifts?"

Martine looked at me, a little surprised, perhaps, at the change in topic. Then she sighed and looked away.

"No, but I can guess," she said.

"Yes?" I prompted.

"She left the party last night with Rubie. I left right after them to go to my scope, so I don't know if they returned to the party or not, but I suspect they did not."

"Oh."

The syllable was as bland as I could make it. I was pleased. Despite this, Martine peered closely at my face. I could feel a flush rushing to my cheeks.

"You know they were involved before?" she asked.

"Yeah. Although after what Theresa told me, I'm surprised that she'd do it again."

Martine shook her head.

"Unfortunately, I'm not. Theresa is head over heels. All Rubie has to do is snap her fingers. Thank God Theresa is leaving tomorrow morning. There's a limit to the damage that can be done."

I continued chopping, not trusting myself to speak. I was hurt, very hurt.

Martine put her knife down. I didn't dare look up.

"What's wrong, honey?" she asked gently.

I shook my head.

"No," Martine stated flatly. "You can't be interested in Rubie."

She put her hand on top of mine, stopping the furious motion of my knife. The tomato I had been slicing was reduced to red sludge.

"I thought Rubie was dancing with Theresa last night," she said slowly, "but the woman was too tall to be her. I should have realized. It was you, wasn't it?"

I nodded miserably.

"Oh dear, dear," Martine said sadly. "Take my advice. Don't let it go any further. Rubie is the last person in the world you should get involved with."

"That's what Theresa said," I added bitterly. "It didn't stop her."

"Rubie is not good for Theresa, but it would be much, much worse for you."

"Why?"

"Because you're Saskia's prodigy."

It was not what I'd been expecting. I looked at Martine blankly. She pushed a bowl at me and instructed me to make brownies.

"You've probably noticed," she began, "that Rubie has some pretty strong feelings about Saskia."

I snorted.

"Okay," Martine continued, "so there's a lot of anger. There's other stuff, too, but it gets buried by the negative feelings."

That matched my assessment of Rubie. I gestured for her to continue.

"Rubie's been up here, waiting for weeks for Saskia to appear so she can confront her. Then you show up with a box full of ashes. She can't yell at Saskia, so to whom do you think Rubie is most likely to transfer those feelings?"

I thought about it. It was obvious.

"Me."

"Right. You. Saskia's favorite."

What a sobering thought. Perhaps it explained the impact of Rubie's presence on me. Delirium is a very rare state for me, and Rubie could induce it with the barest of touches. Her hands were charged with a force that went beyond mere physical attraction. Something else was drawing us together in this strange dance of distance and desire.

"What," I asked carefully, "exactly, is Rubie's deal with Saskia?"

Martine opened her mouth and then shut it.

"Ah, come on," I said, a little exasperated. "What's the big secret?"

"It's not my secret," Martine said.

"How am I supposed to deal with this woman if I don't know anything?"

"I admit you're at a disadvantage," said Martine.

There was sympathy in her voice, but it was clear she wasn't going to tell me what I wanted to know. I threw up my hands in disgust, which sent a fine mist of flour flying through the air. Martine chuckled and passed me the cocoa. Try as I might, I could get no further clues from Martine. She laughingly evaded all my attempts to extract information about Rubie and Saskia. When the brownies were in the oven, I settled on a stool to do some serious thinking.

Were they lovers once? Maybe Saskia had scorned her at some point. But Rubie was several years my junior, making the age difference between them huge. And Saskia had always been involved with men, as far as I knew. Still, stranger things had been known to happen. Perhaps they were rivals. Maybe Saskia had stolen one of Rubie's ideas. But no, Saskia would never have done anything like that. Whatever her faults, plagiarizing was not one of them. She prized originality above everything else.

I just couldn't figure it out. I sat down to dinner, still mystified. I ate automatically, all the while trying to fit together the pieces of this puzzle. When I looked up from my plate, I found myself staring at

Theresa. I returned to the present with a jolt.

Theresa had a wonderful smile on her face. I could tell that she was happy. She'd apparently had a very good time last night. Perhaps Rubie had learned how to fuck more intimately since the last time they'd been together. Theresa turned and caught my eye. She looked instantly apologetic.

"I'm sorry," she mouthed.

I looked away quickly and refused to meet her eyes again. I was more than a little sour with her. I went outside to eat my dessert in peace. It wasn't much of a refuge, though, because a few minutes later, Theresa came out to join me.

"I brought you some coffee," she said, setting a mug down beside me.

I glared at her briefly before returning to my study of the mountains. She sat down anyway.

"I understand if you're mad at me," she said after a while. "I would be, too. And I know what you're thinking: she's a hypocrite and a jealous conniver. Am I right?"

She was, but I didn't reply.

"I feel really bad about what happened. Especially after what I said to you the other day. I can't explain it. Rubie just has that effect on me. I lose every shred of common sense when she's around."

I couldn't really blame her for that one seeing as how I had a similar problem.

"I'd do it differently if I could do it over, but I can't," she said. "Anyway, I'm leaving, and I won't see Rubie again. You will. I hope you two can work something out."

She was sincere. I had to respect that.

"I," I stopped and cleared my throat, "I appreciate that."

She got up to leave. I was struck with a sudden realization: I wasn't really angry with her. I'd done stupid things in my past, too. She might've had poor judgment, but that didn't make her a bad person. No, when it got right down to it, the person I was really pissed at was Rubie. She was jerking Theresa and me around at the same time.

"I wanted to give you this," Theresa said suddenly.

I looked down. In the dim light I could make out the shape of an old-style book. It had a metal spiral at one edge binding the pages together.

"What is it?" I asked.

"It's a diary. It belonged to my many times great-great-aunt Maria. My mother gave it to me when I left the crèche and went to school."

I took it slowly. It was very old, almost brittle.

"I don't understand."

"Maria was an astronomer," Theresa explained. "Almost a hundred years ago, she came to a remote observatory in Chile, a little place called La Vista, to observe a brand new supernova in the Large Magellanic Cloud."

"You're kidding me."

"I'm absolutely serious. She writes about her trip in this book. I thought you might be interested."

"Theresa," I said, stopping her before she could walk away. "I can't take this."

"Please. I want you to. It's a piece of La Vista's history. I know you'll take good care of it. Put it in the library when you're finished."

She did walk away then, leaving me with an incredibly precious gift in my hands. I sat there, holding the diary. After a while, I went back into the hotel in search of Theresa. She was in the common room with Francoise and several other people. Patrique had brought out a bottle of something for a farewell drink. Someone pushed a glass in my hand, and I raised it for the toast. I approached Theresa, still clutching the diary.

"Thank you," I said, giving her a quick little hug.

Her eyes were shining, whether in surprise or something else, I could not tell.

"Thank you, Quincy," she said softly. "Thanks for accepting the apology."

"Have a safe trip," I replied, and quickly escaped.

It was another beautiful night, so I went straight to the dome. While waiting for the scope to finish a sequence, I carefully opened Maria's diary and began to read. Instantly, I was sucked in. I became so engrossed in the diary that more than once I forgot I was running an observation. The scope computers kept me on track, beeping impatiently when I ignored them for too long.

Maria's life had been fascinating. The daughter of a Chilean woman and an American man, she'd been raised in the old city of Santiago. She'd gone to old Boston for a college degree and gotten hooked on stellar astronomy. The supernova of 1987 had brought her back to her homeland. She'd worked on the NTS for almost two months before returning to Boston with her data. Despite her diligent study of one of the most exciting astronomical events of the century, Maria had also made time to observe people. These personal observations were very intriguing.

Some unspoken rule segregates the dining room tables. The tables by the windows are reserved for the astronomers, who are almost all white and European. The other tables are for the support staff, all of whom are Chilean. Within each section, there are finer distinctions. On the astronomers' side, the French and Italians are at the table closest to the food. The next table is for Germans, and so on. On the staff side, the administrators sit closest to the astronomers, followed by the technicians. In the back are the kitchen and janitorial staff. No one else that I've talked to has noticed this. They don't find it strange. "It's not segregation," one man said, "we just choose to sit with people we know."

I never know where to sit. I am Chilean, but I am also an astronomer. I love to hear the lilt of my native tongue, but I also want to talk about my work. Unfortunately, if I sit with the astronomers, the Chilean men think I'm disdaining them, spurning my roots. In return, they are scornful of me. Compounding the problem, I am, out of the two hundred people here, staff and astronomers combined, the only woman. There just aren't many women in astronomy. And they don't hire women staffers here at La Vista. Even the wives of the astronomers have to get special permission to visit their husbands. Staff wives don't come up at all. It's very strange, and it makes me the focus of lots of unwanted attention. I've taken to coming to meals late and eating alone.

In another place she wrote:

> I find it ironic that I'm writing my diary in English. When I am in Boston, I write in Spanish, but here in Chile, the words in my head are English. Of course, English is the lingua franca of science. The astronomers hail from every European country, as well as China, Russia, and Japan, so we must all speak English if we are to understand each other. It is not a particularly pleasant-sounding language, but it is functional. It is the custom of scientists everywhere to speak it. Still, I find it ironic. And disturbing.

I, for one, was glad that she wrote in English. If she'd written in Spanish, I couldn't have read it. When UniTech had brought together the remnants of humanity under its rule, English—the language of science—had become virtually hegemonic. Very few people knew anything else. Maria's discomfort with it, however, was not hard to understand. To speak a foreign language in her native land must have seemed unnatural. Writing her personal diary in a scientific language must have been equally jarring.

Engaging as the diary was, my head was pounding from the strain of reading the loopy handwritten words; my eyes felt dry and sandy. I put the diary aside and called up some music programs from the library computer. I gave the scope equipment the minimal attention necessary and let my thoughts drift.

My thoughts got more and more morose as the night went on. The drama with Rubie had helped take my mind off Saskia, but romance, sordid or not, did not make up for Saskia's absence. I missed her so much. I was in the place she loved best, but she wasn't here. She would have been very excited about this diary. The history of La Vista held a real fascination for her. To see this place through the eyes of a woman astronomer a hundred years ago would have thrilled her. I wished Saskia could have been there to read it with me.

I thought back to Saskia's last day. It had all happened so quickly. One day at the lab she'd gotten dizzy, and I assumed she'd gone home early. I was a little concerned because I knew she had to be feeling pretty bad to leave work. An hour later, I found her wandering in the corridors, completely disoriented. I took her straight to MedCen.

When the results came back that night, I didn't believe them. She couldn't have viral cancer, she just couldn't. The meds assured me that they'd put all their computers to work on engineering a cure. They pumped her full of everything, trying to slow the progress of the virus, but nothing seemed to work.

She had no family and few friends, so I stayed with her all night. She talked to me occasionally, and I was comforted by hearing her voice in the darkness. I had been certain they'd rush in any moment with the cure code, but nothing happened. I sat there, hour by hour, watching as Saskia descended into raving madness, the virus inexorably eating away at her brain. By evening it was over. Twenty-four hours and she was dead.

Now her astronomy papers were also corrupted. It seemed as if I was not allowed to hold on to anything of hers. It was damned unfair.

I sat up suddenly, struck by an incredibly chilling thought. What if the problem with the library was degenerative? What if it was eating away at Saskia's papers bit by bit, like a cancer? I lurched over to the console and logged on to the library. I kept telling myself that it wasn't possible.

I pulled up her first paper, the one that had had a missing reference and turned to the bibliography. I sucked in a painful breath. The blank spot had gotten bigger. Not only was the Gorman reference missing, but Eller, Frank, and Itha were also gone. My throat was tight with panic.

The computer beeped, alerting me that it was getting too light to observe. I responded automatically, closing the dome and shutting down the equipment with a few quick commands. I turned back to the library. I pulled up another paper, the one that had had several scrambled sentences. Now almost every other sentence was mixed up. I went methodically through all of the papers, dreading what I would find. My worst fears were true. The other papers showed similar degeneration. All of Saskia's work was slowly disintegrating, just as she had.

It was unbearable. I got up and stumbled down the stairs. The sun was just edging above the horizon as I set off for the hotel at a dead run.

There were a surprising number of people in the dining room when I burst in: Patrique, Carla, Martine, and others. They'd stayed up to say farewell to Francoise and Theresa. Rubie was there, too, but I was so anguished about Saskia's papers that I didn't have any distress to spare for her. I blurted out my discovery to the group. It came out somewhat garbled, but they got the gist of it. There were grave faces all around the table. They knew it was serious.

"All right. Let's organize," Carla said.

Carla was very good at organizing people. Privately, I thought it was a waste for her to be at La Vista where there were so few people to organize. She would have made an excellent science administrator.

"Patrique, get a software team together. Rouse and recruit anyone who's sleeping. Find out the extent of the damage. Jin-Li, start a full hardware inspection. Martine and Quincy, I want you to devise some place to store the information off the library computer, some place indestructible. Let's get to it. Unless anyone makes any earth-shattering discoveries, why don't we meet back here at 1700."

★

When we stumbled upstairs at 1700 hours, we were no closer to the cause of the disintegration than we had been before. Being up all night and all day had completely worn me out, and it was hard to think straight.

The hardware people had found nothing. The equipment was in perfect shape. Patrique made the software report. So far, only files with Saskia's name attached were affected. The rest of the library seemed intact. Everyone breathed a sigh of relief at that. But Saskia's files were slowly deteriorating. Things that she'd written herself were deteriorating the fastest. Original papers that she had written would be completely unreadable in five days or less. Works that she'd cataloged or anthologized were going more slowly. We had about thirty days before these became inaccessible. In all, almost 20 percent of the library was at risk.

There was silence after Patrique spoke. Finally, Carla called on me and Martine to report.

"We discovered an old recording mechanism downstairs," I said. "We should have it up and running by tomorrow morning."

There was a ragged cheer. Martine held up her hand for silence.

"Celebration is premature at this point. Assuming that we can get it to work the way it's supposed to, and that's still a big assumption, the machine is slow. In addition, we only have a limited number of viable tapes on which we can record data. We can't store the whole library."

"Is there enough room to store everything of Saskia's?" Carla asked.

"Yeah, we should be able to get it all on tape. But not much else," I warned.

"If we can get that stuff on tape before it disintegrates any more, that'll be a real relief," Patrique said.

"Yes, but remember, whatever the problem is, it's going to be stored on the tape, too. The instant you put the info back on line, the deterioration will continue," Martine said.

"Understood," Carla said. "It's a stopgap, not a cure. But let's do it anyway. At least it will give us a little more time."

"Any chance of getting more tapes?" I asked hopefully. "I'd feel safer if we could back up the whole library."

Martine, Carla, and Patrique exchanged a look that I couldn't fathom.

"I'll check on it," Patrique said, finally.

After dinner, Martine and I went back to work. Although I was dead tired, saving Saskia's work was critically important to me, so we kept at it through the night. We were ready for a test run by dawn. Only Martine and I were still awake. I could hardly breathe when we played back the tape. It worked. Martine gave me a big hug. We put a fresh tape in and started recording.

The tape machine was slow. It would take hours to get all of Saskia's original papers backed up. Martine said she could take care of it from there, but I went upstairs to the kitchen to brew some coffee for us instead. I knew I wouldn't be able to sleep until I was sure those papers were safe.

Rubie was in the dining room. She was struggling to hook herself up to the medserver. It was time for her VBC test. I shook my head. It was hard to believe that I'd been at La Vista for a whole week. In some ways it seemed like I'd just arrived yesterday.

"Here," I said, taking the interface out of her hands. "Let me do that. It's hard to do with just one hand."

Rubie jumped a little at my voice. Her back had been turned, so she hadn't seen me come in. I hooked up her wrist access quickly and held it in place.

"It'll just take a minute," I said, avoiding looking her in the eye.

Not a word was spoken in that minute. We both stared at the

computer screen, waiting for the result. As expected, it came up negative. Nevertheless, Rubie put her head down on the table when the *All Clear* flashed on the screen.

"Thank you, Quincy," she said, her voice muffled.

Her childlike sincerity took me by surprise. For a moment, she was completely unguarded. She was not a cold and calculating seductress, just a young woman very worried about dying. My heart went out to her.

"Anytime," I said. "It feels good to even the score."

Rubie raised her head, confusion competing with other emotions.

"The score," I explained, "is now VBC 1, Quincy Alexander 1."

She smiled a little at that. I couldn't help but smile back. I kept warning myself not to start liking her too much again, but it was hard not to respond to that smile. I stood up much too quickly.

"Quincy? Are you okay?"

I gripped the back of my chair and waited a moment for the darkness to go away. When I could open my eyes, I saw Rubie looking at me with concern.

"Fine," I said, moderately convincing. "I just haven't slept in a while. Believe me, as soon as we get those papers on tape, I'm going straight to bed."

I picked up the coffee and waved good-bye before she could protest. The last thing I needed was a lecture on the consequences of extended sleep deprivation.

It caught up with me, of course. All the coffee in the world wasn't going to keep me awake forever. Martine dozed off in her chair after an hour or two. When I knelt to push the last tape into the recorder, the sense of relief was dizzying. I had an idea now how Rubie must have felt when the medserver said she was clear. Knowing you're going to be okay and being okay are two entirely different things. With the relief came exhaustion, this time in full force. The floor suddenly looked incredibly inviting. I dropped down onto it and curled up. The last thing I remember was the wonderfully cool feeling of the tiles against my cheek.

Someone was calling my name from a long way off. I was certain that it was Saskia's voice. I wanted to tell her that everything was okay, the virus was under control, and soon it would be safe for her to come back to life.

I opened my eyes, but it was not Saskia who looked down at me. It was Rubie. Slowly, things reassembled themselves: I was at La Vista, Saskia was dead.

"Thank God," Rubie said. "I thought you'd passed out."

I blinked. I was stuck on that thought—it's not Saskia, Saskia is dead.

"Can you walk? It's only a little ways to your room."

I closed my eyes. I didn't want to deal with it. My dreams were much more pleasant. They invited me back in, and I sunk gratefully down into them. Dimly, I was aware that I was being hoisted by strong arms. I leaned my head into a sweet, soft chest. It smelled like Rubie. Rubie? She couldn't pick me up. She was smaller than I. Then I remembered. She climbed rocks all day; she was very strong.

I woke a little when she laid me down in my bed and pulled the covers over me. I felt the warm press of lips on my forehead, on my nose, and, after a moment, on my lips. I wanted so much to return her kisses, but I was just so tired.

"Don't go," I said.

Why was my voice faint? I was afraid that she wouldn't hear, that she'd leave me by myself. I didn't want to be alone. But she heard. I could feel her sit down on the bed next to me and take my hand. I was so grateful, I wanted to cry.

My body automatically snapped awake at some point, probably dinner time. I thought maybe I should get up, but I was so tired. I became aware of a warm body cupped around mine. I didn't have to feel the wisps of curly hair to know that it was Rubie, sleeping soundly by my side. I snuggled back into her and went to sleep again.

6

The next time I woke, Rubie was long gone. The bed beside me was cool. I almost began to think that I'd dreamed the whole thing. I rolled over to look at the clock. It was nearly noon. I'd slept for close to twenty-four hours. Of course, I'd been awake for the previous forty-eight, so it wasn't that surprising. I felt groggy, but I got up anyway.

A shower and a bite to eat restored me considerably. I wandered over to the library hoping to find Patrique. He was there, tapping away at a terminal. I could tell from his haggard look that little progress had been made while I was sleeping.

"What are you doing?" I asked, hitching a leg up on the desk.

"Quincy!" Patrique said, looking startled.

To my surprise, he jumped up and covered the screen with his hands. I backed away a few feet.

"Sorry to interrupt you," I said, very puzzled.

I must have intruded on something private. I was about to leave when he called me back. He lowered his hands and looked at me apologetically.

"I'm just trying to get a hold of a couple of people who are going to be heading up here in a few days. They can pack in more of those tapes so we can get a hard backup of the entire library."

I considered the implications of what he was saying. Getting a hold of people? That meant electronic mail, and e-mail had to be sent through the Net.

"I thought you didn't have access to the Net," I said.

"We only have limited access," he replied. "No virtual reality at all. Guest account, keyboard access only. Unbelievably slow, but it'll send text."

I watched him for a few minutes.

"Why the secrecy?"

Patrique finished his message and swiveled around.

"Carla, Martine, and I are the only ones who know about this. If we told people here that we had a connect, they'd be wanting to check their mail and contact their friends. But if we use this access point too much, someone at UniTech will notice and start asking lots of questions."

That could be very unpleasant, indeed. Considering UniTech's dim view of pure science, La Vista's intrusions into the Net, however small, would not be welcomed. I didn't want to know what would happen if UniTech found out there was an operational observatory out here.

"So we only use it for emergencies," Patrique continued. "I'd appreciate it if you'd keep this to yourself."

"My lips are sealed," I said.

We discussed what had been discovered while I was sleeping. Although they'd ruled out a lot of things that weren't the cause of the problem, no real progress had been made in determining the culprit. The degeneration continued.

"I don't want to think about what would have happened if you hadn't caught it when you did. What made you go back and check those papers again anyway, Quincy?" Patrique asked.

"It's weird," I said. "I was just thinking about the day she died, and I had this terrible image of viral cancer inside our computer."

"Whatever the reason, I'm glad you did."

"Me, too. I just wish I knew why this was happening."

Patrique shrugged.

"Almost seems like someone has a grudge against La Vista," he said.

It was not something I'd considered.

"You think this is sabotage?" I asked.

"Yes."

"Come on, Patrique. Who would want to do something like that?"

"UniTech," Patrique replied immediately.

I just stared at him for a second.

"Don't you think you're being a bit...," I paused, trying to find the right word.

"Paranoid? For heaven's sake, Quincy, they arrested me for doing a little astronomy on the Net once and you think I'm being paranoid for thinking they might be sabotaging the observatory?"

"But they don't know we're here!"

"Well, maybe they do. Maybe they've learned about this Net access. Maybe UniTech's just started to notice that an amazing number of scientists take holidays in this region. Maybe they have pre-Cat records from this place. I don't know."

I thought about it. It was possible.

"But why now?" I asked plaintively. "And why just Saskia's work?"

"Think about it. Saskia's dead. She was incredibly smart, and very powerful. She could've made UniTech turn a blind eye in our direction. But she's gone now, and we have almost no protection. And, of course, they'd take out her work first. She was always coming up with great new ideas. Besides, she organized the entire library here. If you target anything with her name on it, then you'll wipe out a pretty big chunk of what we know about astronomy."

It was hard to fathom. UniTech had created me, raised me, educated me, and put me to work. Sure it was a huge organization, with all the bureaucracy that entails. It was impersonal, sometimes inscrutable, but UniTech had been instrumental in bringing us out of the Cats. La Vista wasn't a threat to them. And anyway, why would they destroy our library in such a slow, tortuous way when they could just as easily come in with their security forces and unplug it? It just didn't make sense.

I left Patrique in the library and went outside. It was cool but sunny. I sat on a warm rock and looked out over the hills below. It was a brilliantly clear day, but I couldn't see the ocean. Probably too far away.

After a while, I realized that someone was standing beside me. It was Rubie. She was extremely still.

"Hi," I said.

She turned toward me and smiled. Her hair was wet, as if she'd just gotten out of the shower.

"I wondered how long it would take you to notice me," she said.

"Been here long?" I asked.

"Ten minutes," she said, leaning a shoulder against my rock. "You were doing some heavy thinking."

It was good to have company. I'd been working myself into a depression before she'd arrived. I scooted over to make room for her. She jumped up easily and settled by me. I was suddenly acutely aware of the minute distance between her thigh and mine.

"Thinking about home," I said.

"Ready to leave already?" she asked gently.

"In a way. I'd like to see the library safe on tape first, and I'm going to finish Francoise's project. But this place is so full of Saskia—part of me keeps expecting to see her. And then the situation with the library came up. Stars, I thought I was going to go mad until we got her stuff taped."

Rubie reached over and brushed a tear off my cheek. I just shook my head and turned away. I didn't want to cry at that moment. I was tired of crying. After a while, I felt a tentative hand on my shoulder.

"How about a walk?"

I almost refused. I felt like I should be trying to find out what was wrong with the library. The problem was that I didn't have any idea where to start. I was frustrated, angry, and confused. Could it really be a UniTech conspiracy? The whole thing made me want to scream.

"Sure," I said. A walk might help clear my thoughts. They couldn't get much murkier.

Rubie led the way. She stopped from time to time, pointing out flowers and birds. I was impressed by her knowledge. Her keen eyes showed me life in the desert I hadn't even guessed at during the days I'd trudged through the mountains to reach La Vista. At one point, she scrambled up a short but very steep slope. I followed tentatively. Halfway up, I lost my nerve and stopped.

"I don't like this," I said when Rubie peered over the ledge.

"Give me your hands," she said.

"No, I don't think that'll help," I said. She might be a mountain goat, but I certainly wasn't.

"Give me your hands," she ordered more firmly.

Still protesting, I reached up. There was a quick jerk, and suddenly I was standing on the ledge next to her.

"Oh," I said. "Well, thank you."

"Anytime," she grinned.

I paused to brush myself off, but Rubie was urging me forward.

"Look," she said, "boulders!"

There were indeed boulders on the plateau. They came in many sizes, some as big as small houses, but I wasn't sure why they warranted such excitement. Then Rubie skipped up to one and swarmed over it. She jumped down and did it again, this time using a different route.

"Very nice," I said when she came down the second time.

I could tell that this was her natural medium. She was graceful and fluid. Moreover, she was happy. I followed her as she threaded through the boulder field, thoroughly enjoying the way she moved across the rocks. When she beckoned me, I joined her at the base of one of the boulders.

"Try this one," she said.

"Me? Oh, no," I said, backing away. "I couldn't do that."

"This one's easy. It has huge buckets to hold on to. Watch."

Rubie climbed up it in five easy motions. It did actually look like fun.

"Try?" she asked when she was down on the ground again.

"Well, okay," I said, stepping up to the rock.

Instantly, all the handholds disappeared. I stood there, just looking at this big rock. I took a step back and bumped into Rubie.

"Put your hand there. Good, now your other one there. Right. Now step up."

I was off the ground. Unfortunately, I had no idea what to do next.

"Put your left hand there. Good. Bend your leg and put it there. Now just straighten your leg and stand up."

"Ugh," I said.

"Go on. I'm right behind you."

She was. She climbed one step behind me the whole time, telling me exactly what to do at each step. The rock was only a couple meters high, but I felt glorious when I reached the top. I gave a whoop that echoed around the hills.

"Kind of fun, eh?" Rubie said.

"Yes!" I replied with elation.

We walked down the back side of the boulder and went looking for more routes. Rubie explained that each route was a "problem" to be solved, like a puzzle or an equation. You could go to the top, or just traverse around it. Because the boulders weren't far off the ground, we didn't need the protection of climbing gear.

We scrambled over many other boulders together. For a while, the worries of the observatory were far from my mind, and I was absorbed in the pleasure of the rocks. When we finally left the boulder field, I looked back with regret.

"We'll return," Rubie promised.

It was late afternoon. The light was getting softer as we wound our way up to the observatory. The rear of the NTS loomed in front of us, rosy pink.

"Want to watch the sunset from here?" Rubie asked when we reached the base of the NTS.

The sun was just touching the horizon. I agreed enthusiastically. We settled on the ground and leaned back against the column. Neither of us said much. We just sat quietly, as the sky changed colors. Suddenly, I was sad again. It had only been a few sunsets ago that I'd thrown Saskia's ashes from the dome above.

Thinking about that night brought to mind Rubie's strange behavior at the ceremony. I felt much closer to her now, but Rubie's actions were still inexplicable. She was as mysterious as she was compelling. Rubie. Saskia. What was the connection between these two women?

"So what's the deal with you and Saskia?" I blurted out all at once, my curiosity simultaneously overwhelming both my sense of tact and my better judgment.

I regretted my words almost immediately. Whatever attachment there was between me and Rubie was undeniably fragile. Asking probing questions about highly sensitive topics was probably not the best way of cementing a relationship.

A long time passed, and I almost hoped that Rubie was going to pretend she hadn't heard me. Then she shifted from her stony posture and brought her knees up to her chest.

"Saskia," she said slowly, "was my biological mother."

Whatever I had been expecting, that was not it. I stared at her dumbly for a while. Eventually, I remembered to close my mouth and swallow. I grappled for a response.

"She never told me she had a daughter," I said with unfeigned humility. I had arrogantly assumed that Saskia would have told me about anything this significant in her life. Apparently, I was wrong.

"I wasn't her daughter," Rubie said contemptuously. "I was raised in a crèche. The great Saskia wouldn't have anything to do with me after she donated an egg to UniTech's birthing lab."

I shook my head, unable to assimilate all this information.

"She refused to have any contact with me. She was always so busy with her goddamn work. And even when she had a vacation, she couldn't spare an hour for me—she came straight to La Vista. What's a child, anyway, when you have the stars?" Rubie finished bitterly.

It was too much to believe that my dear Saskia could have been this heartless. There had to be another explanation.

"Are you sure?" I asked Rubie. "I mean, mistakes happen. Perhaps the birth records were wrong."

Rubie took in a sharp breath.

"That's what she claimed. She had her secretary write me that once. *You are mistaken, the records are incorrect. Saskia Rushkin is not your mother. Please do not write again.*"

"What about a genetic ID correlation?" I asked gently. "That would have cleared up all doubt."

"Don't you think I tried? Medical records aren't exactly on public access. Saskia would have had to give me permission. The woman wouldn't give me the time of day, much less her g-ID."

Unfortunately, it sounded just like Saskia. She was a stubborn woman. If she'd decided that Rubie was not her daughter, then that was the end of it.

"I'm sorry, Rubie," I said. "It wasn't fair of her at all."

"I didn't want much. I just wanted to meet her, to sit down and have lunch one day. Was that too much to ask?"

"No, it wasn't," I said softly, although I doubted that she was listening to me.

Poor Rubie. Having not felt the same way about my parents, I didn't really understand her passion to know Saskia. But some people were like that. They attached great importance to their ancestry. Privately, I thought such notions were somewhat archaic, especially since birthing technology had essentially separated reproduction from the human body. Nevertheless, I understood frustrated passion very well. Cass had taught me all about that. It hurt. Not only that, it was obsessive—a constant, nagging ache in your heart. No wonder Rubie had been so sensitive to each mention of Saskia's name. Everything made a lot more sense to me now—Rubie's behavior on the trail that first day, her actions at the funeral, her ambiguous feelings for me.

"So I came here," Rubie was rushing on, "because I knew she'd be here. There's nowhere to run to; she'd have to talk to me whether she liked it or not. But the bitch did it again. She went off and died so she wouldn't have to deal with me."

There was nothing I could say. I hung my head and let Rubie rage. She had every right to be angry.

"And you," she cried suddenly, jabbing me with a finger, "you were more her daughter than I was. She taught you, worked with you, told you everything. She loved you, didn't she?"

Each of those last few words was punctuated by a poke in the chest. I caught my breath at the blaze in Rubie's eyes. I felt a great stillness inside as yet more things clicked together in my head.

"Oh my God," I said. "So that's why you went off with Theresa that night. It was revenge, wasn't it? You've been trying to get back at Saskia through me."

I was absolutely appalled. All the warm, fizzy feelings that Rubie had aroused in me soured. I felt like shit. Suddenly, I was incredibly thankful that the sky had cleared that night at the party. If I'd spent the night with her, she certainly would have totally trashed me.

"Well, screw that," I said, seized by anger. "It's not my fault that she loved me. I'm glad she did. I loved her, too. I won't apologize for that. So just go fuck yourself."

I'd gotten two steps before Rubie grabbed me by the shoulder and spun me around. Her face was distorted with tears.

"Let's get two things straight, Quincy Alexander. First, I happen to like you. Despite my better judgment, I find you attractive. That has nothing to do with Saskia."

I drew in a deep breath and let it out.

"What's the second thing?" I asked, unable to keep an edge out of my voice.

"The second thing is that you are just like her sometimes."

I stared at her blankly.

"Think back to that night at the party," Rubie said, half-angrily. "I felt so good in your arms. I couldn't wait to go back to my room and make love to you."

"Yeah, well, that's how I felt, too," I mumbled.

"Then why'd you leave?"

"You know as well as I do," I said. "The sky cleared. I had to go observe."

"Exactly. The stars were calling. And that was much more important than whatever it was we were sharing on the dance floor, wasn't it?"

I bit my lip. She was right. And that's precisely what Saskia had done, abandoned Rubie for the promise of starry nights.

"So I went off with Theresa," Rubie said. "I knew she wanted me more than she wanted to see stars. Revenge? Maybe. I don't know. It wasn't my conscious intent, but I can see how you'd think that."

I went back and sat down at the base of the dome. I pulled up my knees and buried my head in my hands. Rubie settled on my right.

"I'm a shit," I said remorsefully.

Rubie laughed a little.

"Oh, you're not that bad."

"No, really, I've been an asshole to you."

"Well, maybe a little bit. But I've been a bit of an asshole myself when you get right down to it. I'm sure Theresa thinks so."

"Yeah," I grunted. "That wasn't very nice."

"No, it wasn't," Rubie agreed.

"Well, I'm sorry," I said.

"I am too."

"Okay."

I turned my attention back to the sunset, mulling over all that had been said. The horizon was burnt orange. Above and behind us, the sky faded from blue to black. To the right, the first stars were visible. The temperature was dropping fast. I got out my gloves and put on the left one. I gave the right one to Rubie.

"Don't argue," I said, before she could protest. "I won't wear this one if you don't take the other."

She took it and put it on. After a moment, I reached over and touched her bare hand with mine. She held on to my fingers. I pulled her closer so I could tuck both of our hands in my pocket. Soon I felt very warm.

The stars came out. I leaned back to watch the brilliance unfold. Just when I thought there couldn't possibly be any more stars in the sky, more would appear.

I felt a little bereft when Rubie took her hand out of my pocket, but she only did it so she could lay down. She rested her head in my lap. The stars were bright enough for me to see the outlines of her face. Try as I might, I didn't recognize Saskia's features there. I didn't expect to. Saskia had had recurrent melanoma as a young woman, and the surgeries had restructured her face. They had the same color eyes, that was true. But Rubie's nose and chin were strong and sharp where Saskia's had been blunt and smudged with scars. I brushed a few strands of hair out of Rubie's face.

"Flowers of light in darkness," she said, gesturing at the stars. "Watching this, I can almost understand you and Saskia. You're star-crazy."

I leaned over and kissed her, moving lightly across her warm lips. She drew me deeper. I sighed when she let me go, and leaned back against the dome. Every part of my body was shivering. I was hot, I was cold. I was dazed by the stars and the sweetness of that kiss.

The chill wind bit deeper and deeper into my skin. I was stiff with cold, but I could not bring myself to disturb the joy of that place. It was Rubie who finally made us get up and walk. We headed back to the hotel, snaking a path through the domes.

7

We'd missed dinner by more than an hour, so we dug out left-
overs and reheated them. Patrique came in while we were eating.

"Oh, there you are, Quincy," he said. "I couldn't find you anywhere."

"We went for a hike," I explained. "Rubie was showing me how to
climb boulders."

If Patrique wondered how we'd managed to climb boulders in the
dark, his face gave no sign of it.

"Well, Martine and Carla and I are getting together in ten minutes
to discuss this problem with the library computer. Can you join us?"

"Well, I...," I said, glancing over at Rubie. "I have some other things
I need to do."

"We're just going to brainstorm a little," Patrique coaxed. "It
wouldn't take more than an hour. Now that we've got the stuff on
tape, we can relax a little bit and rethink our plan of action. Carla and
Martine think we should try to get back to a more normal schedule
now that the panic is over. You'll still have plenty of time to observe
later tonight."

I bit my lip. Patrique's request was not unreasonable, but I was
loath to break the fragile trust that had sprung up between Rubie and
me.

"Oh, go on, Quincy," Rubie chimed in, unexpectedly coming to
the rescue. "You can spare an hour."

I threw her a grateful glance and agreed to meet Patrique and the
others in the library. When Patrique moved into the kitchen, I turned
back to Rubie.

"Thanks," I said. "I really appreciated that."

"I've had you to myself all day," she said. "Can't be selfish now, can I?"

"It'll just be an hour," I said. "Where can I find you after that?"

Rubie shook her head.

"Don't look for me. Go to your dome and work tonight."

"Maybe I don't want to observe tonight," I said.

This, I figured, was another test. I wasn't going to fail this time.

"Too bad," Rubie said without sympathy. "Astronomy doesn't wait for your whims. You observe when the sun goes down and the weather is clear. That's now. You heard what Patrique said, back to normal."

"But, Rubie, I wanted to spend time with you."

"You will," she said, "but not tonight."

"Stop!" I cried. "I don't understand. You yelled at me before for doing just this."

"This is different," she said primly.

My eyebrows went up in disbelief.

"How so?"

"For one thing, you haven't observed in a couple of nights."

"I don't care," I said stubbornly.

Rubie snorted.

"I don't believe that for a second. And anyway, Quincy," she said, her voice becoming serious, "I don't want to be with you when you're thinking about something else. Let's wait."

"Are you sure?" I asked dubiously.

"Absolutely," Rubie replied firmly. "We'll wait for a cloudy night."

"And when will that be, weather guru?"

She gave me a sly smile.

"Could be soon."

I walked her to her room. She gave me a brief, fierce hug and bid me clear skies. I stood there staring at her closed door for a few moments before I turned and headed to the library.

The meeting was already in progress. There were four of us: Patrique, Carla, Martine, and me. I was the only nonresident present. The topic was Patrique's conspiracy theory. Martine seemed doubtful, but Carla gave it considerable credence. She was, she said, suspicious of any organization that held the entire world under its sway. Technocracy, despotism, oppression—it was all the same to her. We discussed it at length.

"I don't see how any of this is helping us find out what the problem with the computer is," Martine said finally.

"If only we had some idea what we were up against," Carla said, slapping her hands against her thighs in frustration. "That would give us a starting point."

"It's something to do with Saskia," Patrique said. "I'm sure of it. It's just too coincidental. She dies, and suddenly everything starts to unravel."

The silence that followed was grim. We broke for the time being, promising to meet again later. Overall, the meeting was discouraging. There were no new leads. The only place left to look was the system software. But there were billions of lines of code to be searched, and we had no idea what we were looking for besides "something unusual." It was going to take years to get through it all.

Meanwhile, we no longer had an emergency on our hands. There were chores to be done and stars to be studied. We scattered to our various tasks, promising to meet again in the morning.

★

It was a gorgeous, clear night. I slid behind the console at my dome with a real sense of pleasure. Part of me ached to be curled up in bed with Rubie, but I respected the wisdom of her decision. If I were there, I'd almost certainly be thinking about the scope sitting idle while viewing conditions were near-perfect. I went to work with a good heart.

Maria's diary was right where I'd left it. I picked it up again, once the observations were started, and immersed myself between stars. Reading about how Maria fought off the attentions of several different men made the night pass quickly. I was relieved that she did not sleep with any of them. Although she never said anything explicitly, I was convinced Maria was ideal lesbian material.

Toward the wee hours of morning the scope started flashing warning lights at me. It was unable to get a fix on the star whose coordinates I'd input. I put the diary down and gave the scope my full attention. I tried to do the focus manually with no success.

"Shit," I muttered unhappily.

There were two possibilities: scope malfunction or clouds. I prayed for the latter. La Vista's resources were, to say the least, limited. A malfunction could mean big trouble. I thumped down the stairs. Outside, thick bands of darkness cut across the otherwise brilliant night sky. I breathed a sigh of relief. It was only clouds. The nearby domes had already been closed up and shut down. There was probably a crowd of disgruntled astronomers gathering in the dining room at that very moment for an early breakfast. Oh well, it would be nice to have company after a night alone. I circled the dome before going back in to shut down.

The sound of someone coming up the trail made me stop at the door. I was puzzled. People should be going down to the hotel, not coming up to the domes. The pale light of a flashlight passed over my face, momentarily blinding me. When I could see again, Rubie was standing beside me.

"Hi," she whispered. "I couldn't sleep. I saw it was cloudy, so I came up to visit."

She looked like she needed a hug. I gave her one as she leaned into my chest and I squeezed harder. A little groan escaped, and I started to let go.

"No," she said, "don't stop. It feels good."

We stood like that for a long time. Despite the warm meld her body made with mine, I started to shiver. I had left my parka inside. Rubie was shivering, too. I pulled away a little and led her inside the dome.

"I'll just get the scope shut down. Then we can go down to the hotel where it's warm," I said, bending over the console.

Rubie pulled up a chair. After a moment, she ran her hand down my spine, from the base of my neck to my tailbone. Some part of my brain directed my fingers through the last sequence of the shutdown, but the rest of my senses were absorbed in the familiar electricity in her fingertips. The response that she evoked in me was ferocious, delicious, and instantaneous. It was almost frightening.

The light kiss on the back of my neck seemed to follow naturally from the gentle sweep of her fingers. I leaned back into her, not caring about the console or the scope or anything but the light impress of her teeth on my shoulders. I gasped when she took a handful of my hair.

"Easy," she whispered. "Don't pull away. I've got you."

I slowly let out my breath. It was a little scary, but it didn't really hurt. She wasn't yanking my hair, just gently tugging at the roots. It actually felt good. I closed my eyes, willing myself to trust her. She didn't let me down. She worked across my scalp, and nothing else existed except her hands. The feeling of being cared for descended upon me, and I relaxed into the luxury of it.

After an immeasurably long time, her hands moved down, stinging like razors against my nipples. My knees buckled at that, and she eased me down to the floor, cupping herself around me. The hard, cool floor felt delicious against my fevered skin. I could feel Rubie's wonderful teeth on my shoulder, harder now. She held my breasts, touching and teasing until I began to tremble. Suddenly, she was on top of me, unbuttoning my clothes. I closed my eyes as she lowered her mouth to mine. She slipped her hand into my pants, and I heard her moan as she enfolded her hand in the flood of wetness there. Steady and sure, I let go and rode home on a hot flow of joy.

It was dawn when we stumbled out of the dome, leaning heavily on each other. A burst of cold wind stripped me of all the warmth I'd acquired from Rubie. The sky was full of dark, angry clouds. We hurried back to the hotel. We stopped by the dining room on the way to Rubie's room, but I was too giddy to eat more than a few bites of toast.

Once we were inside her room, Rubie guided me into her bed and rolled me on top. Memories of Cass flitted through my head, and I began to panic. I didn't know what to do with a woman underneath me. I had nothing to help me, no electro-stimulators, not even a bottle of lubricant. My whole body went stiff.

"Quincy?"

Rubie's voice was more gentle than I'd ever heard it before. Her body stilled under mine, all playfulness slipping away. I buried my face in her sweater.

"What's wrong?"

"I forgot...," I started, feeling like a miserable fool.

Rubie waited while I swallowed several times. But I couldn't say anything else, and the silence stretched out. How can you forget how to make someone feel good? I'd done it before, I did it to myself all the time, but my brain was stuck on two words: *I can't.* Finally, I made myself look up and meet Rubie's eyes. There was nothing but kindness there.

"Kiss?" she suggested softly.

Yes, a kiss. I remembered kisses. On lips, around ears, down the neck. The best part of the lips for kissing, I recalled after a moment, was that soft, moist part just inside the mouth. Rubie brushed her hand down her chest and across her breasts, so I slowly kissed my way down and lingered there, alternating licks with tiny bites. She rolled over onto her stomach, and I kissed her neck and back until she urged me to put my hand between her legs. Yes, I remembered how to do that, too, picking up slipperiness from the back and gliding forward, around, and back. My heart hammered at every little noise she made.

"Thumb," she said.

So I let my thumb sink in and out with every circle of my fingers. When she started to groan, I held my breath and prayed. The contractions around my thumb spread outward and the rest of her body began to shake. It was that easy. I let my breath out. Rubie flipped over and squeezed me tight, chuckling all the while. I laughed, too, amazed at the simplicity of pleasure.

Being curled in the warmth of Rubie's body was an unspeakable luxury. There was no hurry, no rush. She held me, and it was delicious. I had never found so much enjoyment in being still. From time to time, our bodies slipped into lovemaking or into sleep, but it was her arms locked securely around me that infused me with peace.

Early in the afternoon, Rubie got up to take a shower. Reality took advantage of her absence and snuck back into my consciousness. I never had one-night stands. It's just not something I did. The idea of casual sex was not even remotely appealing to me. I'd never really learned to enjoy sex with people I didn't know and trust. Usually it would take weeks or even months before I was relaxed enough to come at someone else's hands. Yet here I was, getting tangled up with Rubie when I'd known her for hardly a week. The really odd thing was that I was loving every minute of it.

But I had to start thinking about leaving. My job was waiting for me back in New Seattle. I would have to pack up and head down in less than a week. Leaving La Vista. The thought was hard to process. There were so many loose ends—the observing project, the computer problem, and now, Rubie.

Rubie reappeared. Stars, just looking at her made me shiver. I opened the covers and she slid into bed beside me.

"What's this?" she exclaimed as she rubbed my neck.

"What?" I asked.

"These knots in your shoulders," she said. "I thought we got all these worked out. I leave for ten minutes and you get tense all over again."

I grunted a little as she dug hard into one of the tight spots. Her hands were rapidly making me forget what I was worrying about. It had not taken Rubie long to discover that I was a back rub slut. A firm hand on my muscles was all it took to make me relaxed, even goofy.

"I'm sorry," I said contritely.

"What are you thinking about that's getting you tense?" she asked.

"I've got that damn library on my mind," I said, telling only part of the truth. It seemed a little premature to start talking about "the relationship."

"It hasn't been very well-behaved, has it?" she commented.

I snorted.

"Downright rude of it to break down like this," I replied. "I don't know what I'll do if we don't find the problem before I have to leave. Probably worry myself to death over it."

"Don't do that," Rubie said.

We lapsed into silence. Rubie worked my neck and shoulders until my muscles were warm and fluid again.

"Actually, that the library exists at all seems like nothing short of a miracle to me," she said, her hands coming to a stop.

I sighed and rolled over. I'd almost convinced myself to forget about the library, but now Rubie seemed to want to talk about it.

"What do you mean?" I asked, as she settled back down on top of me.

"Well, think about it. You and Martine wore yourselves out getting that tape machine working. It hasn't been used since the Reconstruction. But from what Patrique was telling me, Saskia's been expanding the library for years, inputting all sorts of data and stuff. If she didn't bring tapes, then how'd she do it?"

Rubie had a very good point. I thought about it. The easiest way would have been an automatic data transfer across the Net. But La Vista wasn't on the Net. Then I stopped. We might not have an active node, but La Vista certainly had access to the Net. If Patrique could send electronic mail, and I'd seen him do it the day before, then a data transfer would be simple to arrange.

"Compressed milibursts from the Net," I thought out loud. "She'd only need a second or two to transfer gigabytes of information."

"She must've had one helluva transfer protocol," Rubie added. "That kind of decompression is tricky. One bug in the code could scramble your whole storage system."

My thoughts were racing in a different direction.

"Oh, shit," I said. "Rubie, we haven't even thought about where the library data came from. Maybe the problem isn't here at all. Maybe there's something wrong with Saskia's home directory. My God, her whole life's work is at risk."

"Wait, Quincy, I didn't mean—"

But I was already off and running.

★

I accosted Patrique outside the solarscope, almost out of my mind. I hadn't been in the Net for weeks. What if Saskia's files on the Net were deteriorating as her files in the library were? This was truly terrifying. Saskia's astronomical papers were a treasure and the possibility of losing them was heartbreaking to me. But her work on eco-administration was one of the pillars of the Reconstruction. She'd been the best in the field. If her theories and data were destroyed, the Reconstruction might be set back for decades.

Patrique agreed that we had to find out the status of those files as soon as possible. This definitely qualified as an emergency. We would use the link to the Net.

"I'll need to be able to identify myself so I can scan Saskia's files. That means plugging into my wrist access for my genetic ID."

"Can we use the interface you built for the medserver?" Patrique asked.

"Yes, of course. It should plug right into the machine."

We retrieved the interface and headed for the library. Patrique logged on to the guest account and then helped me tape the interface into the wrist access. I sat down next to him.

"Okay, Quincy," Patrique said. "I'm going to log you on and then transfer control to your keyboard. Get on and off as quickly as possible"

"Got it."

"Go," Patrique said, and I was in.

Virtual reality access made these kinds of tasks much quicker, but we didn't have anything like that. Keyboards are slow; there's just a limit to how fast human fingers can move. Still, I was pretty fast. Once the Net had confirmed my identity by querying the genetic ID in my IMC, I was able to run an integrity program on all the files in Saskia's home directory. The result came back in two minutes: no damage. Thank God. I paused for half a second to enjoy the rush of

relief and elation. Then I scrammed. I logged off and removed the interface from my wrist. Not more than five minutes had elapsed.

I could feel adrenaline pumping through me. It was making me
high. My exhaustion had disappeared, and I wanted to go out and
climb mountains. I felt tremendously pleased with myself. I spun
around in my chair, grinning hugely.

"There!" I exclaimed with gusto. "Was that something?"

My senses were abnormally sharp and clear. The colors in the room
suddenly struck me as incredibly vibrant and intense. I could pick up
the minute sounds of the heating equipment. The earthy smell of the
greenhouse several stories below tickled my nostrils. I started to laugh.
I'd never felt more alive.

Patrique was peering intently at my pupils.

"Quincy," he said, his voice strained with worry, "are you okay?"

Laughter continued to boom out of me.

"Okay? OKAY! I'VE NEVER FELT BETTER!" I shouted.

Prepared to rush out and scale the highest mountains, I leapt up
from my chair and kept going right through the roof. I went higher
and higher until I was flying through the clouds. I caught a jet stream
and coasted around the world before turning back to the sky. The
stars beckoned, and I flung myself into the darkness.

I could no longer fly when I woke. It was a disappointment, to say the least. Suddenly, Martine's lovely face obstructed my view of the ceiling. It was something of a consolation.

"How are you feeling?" she asked, putting her hand on my forehead.

Besides thinking I was unfairly grounded, I didn't feel half bad.

"Okay," I said. "Where am I?"

"You're in your room."

I swung my legs over and sat up.

"Dizzy? Sick to your stomach?" she asked.

"I'm starving," I said. "What happened?"

"You've been out for less than an hour. We're not sure how, but your IMC got reprogrammed while you were logged on. It told your body to start producing adrenaline, endorphins—all sorts of nice things. It got you high."

"How did you bring me down?"

"We wiped your IMC."

I looked at her in alarm.

"My IMC's empty?"

That was a frightening thought. Without the software, my IMC was just a worthless piece of subcutaneous hardware. My little old immune system could never protect me from virals by itself.

"No, no, don't worry," Martine said. "You put your medical software into our medserver when you were testing us for the VBC, remember? We just fed it back into you."

The medserver was sitting next to my bed, blinking reassuringly.

"Glad you thought of it."

"I walked into the library just as Patrique started to panic. He thought he'd killed you."

"Well, I'm alive, and hungry as a black hole," I said.

"All right, all right," Martine laughed. "At least you don't seem to be suffering any side effects. Here, put on some clothes before you go."

Martine wheeled the medserver out in front of us. I got a small cheer when I walked into the dining room. Apparently, news of my adventure had spread. Rubie ran up and threw her arms around me, promising to throttle me if I ever did anything that stupid again. Patrique and Carla got up to give me a hug. I suffered their poundings and sat down to eat.

When dinner was finished and the table cleared, Patrique, Carla, Martine, and I sat down again to discuss the day's events.

"I think Quincy's experience proves there is a UniTech conspiracy," said Patrique, who was sitting across from me.

I just looked at him.

"Think, Quincy. Your IMC was reprogrammed from the Net. Who do you think has the power to do that?"

"Only Medical Central."

"Right. And UniTech runs MedCen."

"But why would they want to reprogram my IMC?" I asked plaintively.

"That drug sequence on your IMC was the first part of a patterning," Patrique explained. "It's a standard procedure to wear down your mental resistance. If you'd been on any longer, you'd have gradually become more and more biddable. Someone at UniTech would then start asking you questions. *Where are you? What are you doing?* And you'd answer with complete honesty. It's more effective in virtual reality, but they can manage with text-only screens like ours, too."

I stared at him in horror.

"They can't do that," I said.

"Oh, yeah? How do you think I got caught doing astronomy?"

I was too stunned to say anything.

"UniTech has considerable license when it comes to tracking down Net criminals," Patrique continued. "Take it from me."

Carla swore profusely.

"I had no idea," murmured Martine.

Several moments passed in silence. I digested the information with difficulty. The prospect of having UniTech as an adversary was overwhelming. It was just too big to fight. There was not much more to say.

I wandered over to the library after the meeting. Carla had not assigned me a chore. My job, she had said, was to rest and recuperate. I was grateful for the exemption. The library was disheveled from days of frantic activity. The paper books, however, sat in their book-cases, completely undisturbed by the recent panic. That reassured me somehow.

I sat down at a terminal without touching the keys. I was pro-foundly disturbed. What was UniTech doing? There could be no doubt that they were the ones reprogramming my IMC. That, in itself, was terrifying. But what frightened me even more was that they knew who I was. I had used the genetic ID in my IMC to get access to Saskia's files on the Net. UniTech would be able to trace that instantly. They had my name. Whatever the trouble was, I was right in the middle of it.

"Hiya, gorgeous."

I looked up to see Rubie hitching herself up on the table. She was very good at sneaking up on me unawares.

"I just had a great idea," she said. "Why don't we take off for a couple of days? There's a terrific place to climb about half a day's hike from here. We could go out tomorrow, camp out there, come back the day after. It's very pretty. I could show you more about climbing, and you'd only miss one night of observing."

It was tempting, very tempting. Just pack up and run away into the wilderness.

"I don't think so, Rubie," I said.

"Ah, come on. Why not?"

"I have a lot of work to do," I replied.

"Don't be so uptight. Relax for a little while. Have fun."

Rubie's playfulness was exacerbating my headache. I just shook my head.

"What's wrong?" she asked.

I closed my eyes. Everything was a mess, and I didn't want to drag Rubie into it.

"I just need to work some stuff out here," I said, and stopped as my voice cracked on the last word.

"Oh."

A minute passed by in silence. I was too wound up in my misery to say anything.

"Well," Rubie said finally, "I guess I won't bother you any more."

"Rubie, I'm sorry, I—"

"Don't explain," she said, standing up. "It's clear where your priorities are."

I rapidly reevaluated my plans. Rubie was not a child. I was not doing her any favors by trying to protect her from the truth. She'd just resent me for it.

"You don't understand," I said, intending to tell her everything. "Something's come up. Let me explain."

"What's there to explain? Love and astronomy don't mix. Well, fuck you, too."

"No, wait! Rubie!"

She was already out the door. I ran after her, through the dining room and out the door. Rubie had already disappeared into the darkness, and the sound of her footsteps faded even as I listened for them. I didn't have my flashlight. There was no way I would find her.

I groped my way back to the hotel. My headache was raging. I couldn't believe what had just happened. Rubie was so damned sensitive about certain subjects. She hadn't even given me a chance to explain. Now she hated me. My misery was complete. I stumbled down to my room and collapsed on the bed. I was too weak and dispirited to get up and get a pain relief program from the medserver, so I just lay there with my pounding head, crying into my pillow and suffering extremely.

A light tap on my door woke me. I must have dozed off, although it was hard to imagine how considering the pain in my head.

"Come in," I croaked out.

If it wasn't Rubie, I was going to start crying again.

"Quincy?"

It was Rubie.

"Yeah," I said gruffly. "Don't turn on the lights. My head hurts too much."

I also didn't want her to see my red eyes and puffy face. I was not one of those people who can cry elegantly. Rubie came over and sat on my bed.

"I'm sorry," she said. "I don't know why I lost it like that. It was totally uncalled for. I should have talked to you about it instead of storming away."

So Rubie had decided to act like an adult. I was impressed. And relieved. It was definitely her turn to be mature.

"It didn't feel very good," I said, just a little petulant. "I'm not used to people exploding at me like that."

"I wasn't angry with you," Rubie said, sighing heavily, "even though that's how it came across. You didn't do anything wrong. I reacted poorly. When you said you had too much work to do, it brought up all that stuff with Saskia again."

"I'm not Saskia," I said emphatically, wondering how many more times we were going to have to go through this.

"No, you aren't."

"I like you a whole lot, Rubie," I continued. "I have an incredible amount on my mind right now, but that doesn't mean I don't want to spend time with you."

She crawled onto the bed and nestled herself next to me. I gave her a long hug.

"Thanks," she whispered after a while. "I appreciate that. I just wish you didn't have to leave."

"I may not be leaving any time soon," I said with a sigh, all my worries returning in a rush.

Rubie twisted around in my arms.

"What are you saying?"

I explained to her about UniTech having my g-ID. Even in the dim light, I could see her face become grave and still.

"Oh, God, Quincy. What are you going to do?"

"Try and figure out what's going on," I said with a shrug. "Maybe Patrique's wrong."

Rubie was quiet for a long time.

"What is it?" I asked finally.

She blinked and shook herself slightly. "What's what?" she replied.

"I don't know. You just looked like you were going to say something. What were you thinking about?"

She buried her head in my chest.

"No, I wasn't thinking of anything in particular. Just spacing out," she said, her voice muffled by my shirt.

I held her like that until she fell asleep. Gingerly, I edged out from underneath her. She rolled away from me, but the steady breathing continued. I pulled the blankets over her and slipped out of the room.

★

I was more determined than ever to find the cause of the problem in the computer. I firmly resolved to go through every line of code in the entire system if that's what it took.

The library was full of people. I knew I would not get any work done if I stayed there, so I headed up to my dome. I could log on remotely to the library from there.

For a long time, I just sat by the terminal, thrumming my fingers on the edge of the table. I was glad that the Net files were safe, but I was frustrated beyond belief. Saskia's astronomy files were getting more and more scrambled with every passing second. It seemed that La Vista's computer system was uniquely cursed.

Something was bothering me, some little detail tickling the edges of my awareness. I shook my head, trying to rattle the idea out. Something about scrambling the library. Yes. What was it Rubie had said about decompressor protocols? One bug and it scrambles your whole data storage system. I straightened up to the terminal and put my restless fingers to work on the keyboard.

Six hours later, I was looking at the origin of the deterioration. It wasn't exactly a bug, just an ambiguity in the umpteenth iteration of a minor algorithm in the decompressor. Saskia had forgotten to specify the overflow bin number, leaving the computer to choose its own. I concocted a high speed simulation and ran the algorithm through it. Sure enough, after about fifty thousand iterations, the algorithm slowly started to eat away the data storage units. The degeneration was almost identical to what I'd seen in the library.

After the agony of the past week, my discovery was almost anticlimactic. A minor omission in an auxiliary program was the cause of all our trouble. I shook my head, amazed by the simplicity of it, and shut down the decompressor. That was that, no more crisis. Yet one little thing still nagged at me: how had Rubie known?

★

The dining room was empty, but Martine was in the kitchen. She looked up from her tea as I came skidding into the room. I blurted out the news.

"Fantastic!" she said enthusiastically. "Great work, Quincy."

"It was all Rubie's idea," I said, grinning. "I've got to go find her and tell her that she saved the day."

I also wanted to know where a so-called climbing bum learned so much about decompressors. I was starting to suspect that Rubie Marle had a few more secrets.

Martine stopped me before I got even a few steps.

"Rubie's not here, Quincy. She left on a camping trip about an hour ago. She asked me to tell you she said good-bye."

I felt like I'd been poleaxed. I sunk into a chair.

"Did she say how long she'd be gone?" I asked when I could speak.

"Not long," Martine said reassuringly. "A couple of days. She said she had some thinking to do and wanted to be out in the mountains."

I mumbled something to Martine as I headed to the dining room. I sat down in the first available chair and stared out the window. I couldn't believe that Rubie would just leave like that, without saying a thing to me. I thought we'd worked through things. I shook my head. There was no way to know what was wrong until she got back.

As I got up to leave, I noticed that the medserver was sitting in a corner of the room. I wondered idly what it was doing there. Perhaps someone had gotten sick. The power was still on. It wasn't good to wear out the power packs like that if no one was using it. I was about to put it on standby and roll it back to its charging station across the hall when I noticed Rubie's name on the screen. She had been the most recent user. She'd been using it the previous night, just before she'd asked me to go camping. That got me a little worried. What if she'd gotten sick?

I sat down at the machine. I needed to know if Rubie was okay. Probably she had just dialed up a pain relief code or something. I logged on and asked for a summary of the most recent procedures.

What I saw did not make sense. Somehow, Rubie had accessed the personal medical records stored inside the server. How she had bypassed the security on those files, I had no idea. I didn't know how to do it. Certainly no climbing bum should have been able to do it. Nevertheless, Rubie had. I scrolled backward, trying to figure out why she would have wanted to look at other people's medical histories. Then I saw it: two g-IDs linked by a correlation algorithm.

It all became clear to me. My doubts about UniTech's parenting records had infected Rubie. But she'd been one step ahead of me. I hadn't even considered the medserver. Anytime anyone used a medserver, their g-ID was read and recorded, just as mine had been when I entered the Net. During her many visits here, Saskia must have used this medserver. Her g-ID would be registered. And I knew Rubie's was, since I'd put it in myself when I was testing for the VBC. So Rubie had decided to break in and run a correlation algorithm on their IDs to see if they really were related.

Although I knew it wasn't exactly the most ethical thing to do, I ordered the medserver to redo the correlation. I had to know what Rubie had found. I watched anxiously as the running correlation coefficient was displayed on the screen. The size of the coefficient indicated the degree of similarity between the two g-IDs. The coefficient got bigger and bigger until it reached fifty percent—the parent percentage.

I turned away from the screen, not sure what my feelings were. In a way, I was glad that Rubie was vindicated. It gave her bitterness some meaning. On the other hand, it meant that Saskia had done something very cruel, almost unforgivable. That act blighted my bright memories of her.

With a sigh, I turned around to shut down the medserver. I sat stock-still in amazement when I saw the screen. The coefficient continued to increase. Seventy, eighty, ninety, one hundred percent. One hundred percent correlation meant that the two gene codes were identical.

"I must have made a mistake," I muttered, looking back at the correlation algorithm.

I reran the algorithm. Same result. Something must have gotten mixed up somewhere. I ran the correlation again, using my ID instead of Rubie's. This time, the coefficient was much less than one percent, not anywhere big enough to be statistically significant. I recalled both Saskia's and Rubie's ID and did it again. The result was as before. One hundred percent correlation. I ran every conceivable test I could think of and nothing changed.

It was impossible. The only people who had matching g-IDs were identical twins. And Rubie and Saskia couldn't be twins—there was forty years difference in their ages. The medserver was broken. It had to be. It was the only explanation. Not unless—I stopped in mid-thought and drew in a long, unsteady breath—not unless the rumors were true.

The story came around periodically, picked up and circulated around the laboratory grapevine by excitable young researchers. Someone in the bio-engineering lab allegedly leaked the information: UniTech was making human clones. There were long arguments in our lab about why anyone would want to do such a thing. The consensus was that they did it to preserve the genes of brilliant scientists who were indispensable to the Reconstruction.

Once I made the mistake of joking with Saskia about it, saying that she was an ideal candidate for cloning. "Wouldn't want to lose your genes," I cracked. Her response to this was one of the most brutal tongue lashings I ever received. *Liar, traitor, gossip-monger*— she called me all these things and accused me of insulting her in the most base way possible. The idea of cloning repulsed her. "Clones," she shouted, almost frothing at the mouth, "are unnatural and obscene." I was so astonished, it was all I could do to stammer out apologies. I was shaky for days afterwards.

At the time I had been sufficiently cowed to banish thoughts of cloning from my head. In retrospect, however, Saskia's vehemence was suspicious, damning even. I stared at the computer screen. The evidence was right there in front of me. It made sense. UniTech obviously knew all about cloning. Much as Saskia hated the idea, she hadn't been able to prevent them from cloning her genes. She was far too valuable not to clone. Rubie was the result.

I closed my eyes. Poor Rubie. She never had a chance. Saskia had hated her before she'd even been born. That's why Saskia had refused to see her. She'd hated the very idea of Rubie's existence.

I jumped at the sound of someone clearing her throat nearby. I jerked my head around to see Martine standing right behind me, looking over my shoulder. Hastily, I cleared the screen and shut down the machine, but not before Martine had seen what was there. Curiously, she did not look surprised, or even disturbed.

"Come on, Quincy," said Martine, patting my shoulder. "Let's take a walk. I want to tell you a story."

She walked to the door and I followed, unresisting. We headed up the main trail toward the scopes. After several minutes of moving in silence, Martine began to speak.

"Forty years ago, I was a young medical researcher, just out of school. It was in the middle of the Second Cat, and we were working like maniacs to get people fitted with IMCs. We knew that there would be side effects, but the IMCs were the only things that impeded the virals, so we installed them indiscriminately.

"Unfortunately, the constant stream of antibodies that the IMCs stimulated had an effect on body chemistry. We began to realize that the reproductive system was the most sensitive to these changes. Humans became sterile. We couldn't live without the IMCs, that much was clear. So MedCen started cloning. You belong to one of the last generations of egg-sperm babies. Rubie does not. She was cloned from Saskia's cells."

"Wait a minute," I said, my head whirling with this onslaught of information.

Martine waited while I sorted through that huge revelation.

"So you're saying that we're all sterile?" I asked, incredulous.

"Every last one of us. Cloning is the only method of reproduction that humans have left."

It was almost impossible to fathom. If I hadn't done the correlation myself, I wouldn't believe it. I wasn't sure I believed it anyway. Maybe the high altitude was making us all crazy. I had never imagined a problem of this magnitude.

"But why doesn't anybody know about this?"

Martine shrugged.

"UniTech feared, not unreasonably, that there would be widespread panic. Our survival is such a fragile thing. The illusion of normalcy is vital. How do you think people would react if they found out that their children were actually monsters of bio-engineering?"

"Surely they'd still love them," I said.

"You think so? Saskia certainly didn't."

I stopped walking. We had passed all the lower domes. Up ahead was the NTS and, beyond that, the radioscope. Below us, clouds were rolling in from the west, lapping against the sides of the mountains like ocean waves. I had never been above the clouds before. They were really marvelous to watch. I stared at them, wishing I could fill my mind with clouds instead of having to listen to Martine.

"Saskia was a hard woman," I said softly, almost to myself, "but she had a lot of love inside. She was like a mother to me."

"Yes, to you. You were normal. Rubie wasn't. Saskia didn't think that clones were real people."

We continued up the trail, past the NTS and down the other side. I chewed my lip as I walked, trying to sort out my thoughts.

"How come nobody's noticed that the world's full of clones?" I asked after a while.

"Each clone's IMC is programmed slightly differently. Minor changes in hormones in the first years of life can radically alter the appearance of the adult. When a parent visits his or her child in the crèche, they see a definite resemblance, but there's enough difference that they don't suspect the truth. Besides, people don't see what they don't expect to see."

"Does Rubie know?"

"That she's a clone? If she believed the correlation, and I think she did, then yes."

"So that's what she needed to think about," I said. "Did you tell her the rest of it? About the sterility?"

"Oh, no. I didn't speak to her at all. I just saw her working at the medserver last night and drew my own conclusions. I didn't think it would help her to know the other stuff."

I thought about that for a minute.

"So why did you tell me?" I asked.

We had come to a halt at the bottom of the small valley between the NTS and the radioscope. Martine fumbled in her pocket for something. At last, she held up her flashlight.

"You see, my young friend, Saskia left a legacy of sorts up here at La Vista. She was going to show it to you on this trip. But she died before she could do that, so it's up to me to pass it on to you. God knows, I don't want to have to worry about it anymore."

"If there's any kind of inheritance," I said firmly, "then Rubie should get it."

"You can pass it on to Rubie if you want. I personally wouldn't recommend it. But wait and see what it is. Then you can make your decision."

With an incredibly smooth motion, Martine vaulted up to a small ledge more than a meter above the trail. Slightly daunted by this display of agility, I scrambled up in a far less dignified manner. It seemed that everyone on this mountain besides me was an Amazon.

"I may be old enough to be your mother," Martine said, pulling me up the last little bit, "but I can jump like an old goat."

I snorted a little at that and paused to dust myself off. When I looked up, Martine was gone.

"Martine?"

"In here," came a voice from a crack in the rocks.

I went over to the dark space and looked in.

"Come on. Don't just stand out there," Martine said from inside. Luckily, my flashlight was right where it should have been. I pulled it out of my pocket before sliding gingerly into the crack. Martine was standing a meter or so from the entrance. I played my light in all directions. We were in a long, narrow cave. It was about two meters across, six meters high, and longer than my flashlight would reach.

Martine moved off, and I followed as close behind as I could without actually stepping on her heels. I noticed after a while that the path on which we were walking was well-worn. It was cool and dry. Martine stopped so abruptly that I walked right into her.

"Sorry," I said, backing up a few feet.

In front of us was a thick steel door with a g-code lock. Martine touched her access to it. A small green light on the lock flashed and the door slid open smoothly.

"Touch your wrist access, too," she said.

I obeyed, and the light blinked red.

"Once more," she said.

I did it again, and the light flashed green again.

"My access has been deactivated," Martine said. "You are now the only person who can get through that lock."

I stepped through the doorway, wondering why I would want to come through it again. I considered asking Martine, but she was clearly enjoying the intrigue. I decided to let her have her fun. I had a feeling I would find out what this was about all too soon.

The door closed behind us. Martine turned off her flashlight.

"Lights!" she called out.

It was quite dim, but it was definitely light. After a few seconds, I noticed that it was getting brighter. In a minute, it was as light as a sunny day.

"That way it doesn't blind you after coming through the cave," Martine said.

"Clever."

We were in a short tunnel with walls of smooth steel. There was another door at the end of it, and we went through a procedure similar to what we'd done at the first one. We stepped into a small room. There were computers all along the back and side walls. Martine sat down at the control panel in the center of the room while I went to look out the huge glass door at the front. It seemed to be a cold storage room. At least there was lots of cold-looking mist swirling around inside. It gave no other indication about its nature.

"What's in there?" I asked, pointing to the door.

"Human embryos," she said, without looking up.

Martine was sitting in the only chair in the room, so I sat on the floor. This was simply too much to process all at once, and I suspected there was more to come.

"It doesn't make any sense," I said, even though it was beginning to.

"It's Saskia's private collection. She started acquiring them very early on, when there were still viable gametes in the sperm and egg banks. She made embryos and then froze them. It was her life's passion."

"No," I said firmly, holding on to this one last shred. "Astronomy was her passion. She always said that."

"Astronomy? Or La Vista? Don't confuse the two. There's a lot more to La Vista than star-gazing."

I *was* confused. I couldn't remember now which Saskia had said. She had spoken frequently and eloquently of the wonders of La Vista, inspiring in me an overwhelming desire to see the place.

"In fact," Martine continued, "astronomy as we know it here at La Vista owes its existence to Saskia's obsessive dislike of clones."

"This observatory existed long before we were born," I argued.

"Oh, yes, but it was in a sad state when Saskia rediscovered it twenty years ago. She put a lot of effort into this place. Over the years she's recruited hundreds of people. And while everyone else was busy building the greenhouse and the generator and the pump, Saskia was down here."

"Just where is here?" I asked, looking around.

"We're about thirty-five meters directly below the NTS. This once was a liquid nitrogen storage facility for the NTS. Saskia converted it into a refrigerated storage unit and brought her embryos. It runs off the power generator. And the love of astronomy draws a steady stream of competent volunteers, so the generator is constantly maintained."

I got up and started walking around the room. The enormity of Saskia's secret life was impossible for me to grasp. On the one hand, I did not think that Martine would lie to me. On the other, I hadn't thought Saskia would have either.

"Patrique," I said. "What about Patrique? He's not exactly what I'd call a volunteer."

Martine sighed and shook her head.

"Well, that was Saskia's doing, too," she said sadly. "She'd been trying to get him to move up here for years. He's a very competent astronomer, and a good fix-it person. Just the kind of full-time guardian La Vista needs. Anyway, Patrique was reluctant to leave his job and his friends permanently, so Saskia made the break for him. She more or less encouraged him to use the Net for astronomy and, when he was caught, she made sure he got the stiffest penalty possible. He came here, just as she'd planned."

"Does Patrique know this?" I asked.

"Of course not. In fact, he's grateful to her for offering him La Vista as an alternative. She rescued him from a joyless existence."

"But you and Carla have been here for years," I protested. "Surely you know La Vista better than Patrique. And you like being here. You came by choice. You two make ideal guardians."

Martine had a sad smile on her face.

"Ah, but we're women, and old women at that. La Vista has far too many women. Saskia wanted a man."

"But this is almost like a sanctuary for women. I thought maybe Saskia discouraged men from coming here so we could have a place of our own."

Martine barked out a bitter laugh that bore no resemblance to her easy chuckle.

"Oh, Quincy. You are very sweet. I'm actually sorry to have to tell you these things. No, Saskia didn't mean for this to be a sanctuary. Far from it. She practically begged men to travel to La Vista. But only the women came. Patrique was the sole man who even visited."

"But why? I don't understand."

I was thinking back to the diary that Theresa had given me. Maria had struggled mightily as the sole female among hundreds of male staff and astronomers. *There just aren't many women in astronomy*, she'd written. Things had certainly changed.

"Why? It's actually very simple. Astronomy is looked down upon these days. There's no money, no prestige, no rewards. That automatically makes it women's work."

It was the truth. The Reconstruction had brought women and people of color into science and technology like never before. The Cats had so radically decimated the population that UniTech could afford to encourage and educate everyone to take part in the new, Earth-oriented sciences. Still, inequalities remained, and gender was among the most persistent categories of difference. Saskia had been one of the few women to become a really high level science adminis-trator in UniTech.

"Why did Saskia want men so badly?" I asked.

Martine shrugged.

"Hard to say. Maybe she thought La Vista needed a father figure, a leader for the harem. Who knows?"

The picture that was emerging of my beloved Saskia—so ruthless and manipulative—was breaking my heart. I wanted to vomit.

"I hate this," I cried, swinging my arm to encompass everything. "I hate it. How could she do this, Martine?"

Martine waited before replying. When she spoke, her voice was quiet and soothing.

"She saw herself as a savior, Quincy. Nothing less. Clones weren't real people to her, they weren't human. She believed that the salvation of humanity depended on preserving those embryos."

"But what was she preserving them for?"

"For the end of the Reconstruction, the day when the earth was clean. No more pollution, no more virals—an Eden where people could live in purity and breed to their hearts' content."

Martine's tone was nothing short of contemptuous. I, too, was scornful of such a dream. It was an arrogantly heterosexual fantasy of reproduction. Saskia had been hidebound in many ways, and her reverence for heterosexuality was one of those failings. I had recognized it in her before, but I'd never dreamed it would have the ramifications I saw before me now.

"What was Saskia thinking?" I wondered out loud, beginning to pace the room again. "The Reconstruction won't end in the foreseeable future. These embryos will be sitting here for a thousand years."

"A thousand? Try a million, or two million years."

I looked at Martine blankly.

"It's the truth, Quincy, another truth UniTech thinks that the public can't bear to know. Humanity screwed up really bad. We're doing all we can, but the biggest part of the Reconstruction will be waiting for the earth to heal itself. That takes time."

"A million years?"

"At least. Look here," Martine said, thrusting out her arm and pointing to her IMC. "We're modifying ourselves already. And it's just the beginning. The whole concept of what it means to be human is changing irreversibly. In a million years, those poor little things in that freezer will be sadly outdated."

I kicked the wall, and was rewarded with shots of pain in my foot.

Reinforced steel was not the best target for anger. I hobbled over to the glass door and pounded on it with my hand.

"This is disgusting," I shouted. "Oh, Saskia, what a fucking waste."

I whirled on Martine.

"You knew all about this, didn't you? If it's so abhorrent to you, then why didn't you try to stop her?"

Martine gave me that sad, weary smile.

"I tried. Maybe I should have tried harder, Quincy. I don't know. I love the observatory too much. Surely the privilege of doing astronomy was worth the price of this abomination."

I thought about it. It didn't take me long. Martine was right. The observatory was the important thing. It didn't matter if Saskia had only done it as a cover. It was still a great achievement.

"So what are you going to do with it now?" I asked quietly, my anger spent.

"Me? I'm not going to do anything. It's up to you now. The main computer is now keyed to your g-ID. You can do anything you want with it. I won't mention it ever again."

Before I could find my voice, Martine had gotten up and slipped out. I started to follow her, but I stopped before I got to the door. In spite of my feelings of disgust, I was slightly curious. I went over and sat down at the terminal.

The first thing I did was to inquire about the size of this facility. Just how many little critters were we talking about, anyway? The number came up immediately. Half a million embryos. It was a significant fraction of the entire human population. I gasped. There was simply no other appropriate reaction.

After I recovered from the shock, I began to explore the rest of the system. It was a straightforward cold storage device. Shutting it down would not be difficult. A simple four-stroke key sequence. My fingers lingered over the keyboard. I was tempted to turn it off without another thought, but that seemed too rash. I pushed myself away from the terminal. The day had already held too many surprises. I knew I wasn't thinking clearly, that I needed to slow down before I did anything about this legacy of Saskia's. I logged off and escaped back through the cave.

9

It was surprisingly warm and pleasant when I stepped from the cave. My eyes watered with the brightness of the sunlight, but it felt good to be out of that tomb. Yes, that's what it had seemed like back there: a cool, steel-lined tomb.

I hiked to the NTS and sat down, my back pressed against the base of the column. It was only a few days since Rubie and I had sat here, talking and fighting and kissing. The last thought sent a shot of warmth down my spine and through my crotch. I wished Rubie were with me now. I hoped fervently that she was all right. Come back, I thought fiercely, come back and we'll comfort each other, Rubie.

Finally, I cried. The tears had been building in me since Martine led me to that terrible place in the mountains. I had lost Saskia yet again, this time in a way more profound than her actual death. I had lost my belief in her perfection; I had lost my love. The woman that I had loved—the passionate astronomer—was a lie. She was just a human being, and a stupid, arrogant, heterosexist one at that.

I stopped crying eventually. The warm breeze dried the wetness on my face. I sat there, staring blankly out at the desert mountains, so desolate and beautiful. My heart was empty.

The sound of footsteps broke my reverie. For one wild moment I thought it was Rubie. It wasn't. In fact, it was nobody I'd ever seen before. It took longer than it should have for it to register that the person approaching me was wearing the blue uniform of UniTech security. The guard's hand rested lightly on her holstered stinger. I got up slowly.

"Who are you?" asked the guard.

It had all happened so quickly that I didn't even think to tell a lie. "Quincy Alexander."

"Please come with me, Dr. Alexander. We've been looking for you."

Don't ask me why I ran. Perhaps I had some wild thought of finding Rubie and escaping into the mountains. Of course, it was impossible. I hadn't gotten two steps before I realized that there is absolutely no place to hide in the desert. Even if the guard had not been stronger and faster than I, she had a stinger. I'd gotten about three meters before she stung me. I went sprawling. The intensity wasn't enough to knock me out, or even paralyze me—it just stopped me from running. I lay there with my face in the dirt, listening to the guard approach. She drew me to my feet with surprising gentleness and began to brush me off.

"Look, Dr. Alexander," she said, "I can sting you unconscious and carry you back, or you can walk."

I stared at her. Her name, according to her badge, was Sergeant Fawks. She did not look brutal by any means. Nevertheless, I was absolutely certain that she would do as she told me if I made it necessary.

"I'll walk," I said.

The guard did not draw her weapon again. She walked behind and to the left of me, directing me toward the hotel.

They had found me. Impossible as it seemed, UniTech had found me. I never dreamed that they would come to La Vista in search. A stupid assumption. My vacation plans of "hiking in the Andes" pointed directly to La Vista for anyone who knew where and what it was. Apparently, UniTech knew.

We walked in silence for most of the way. There were guards scattered everywhere, the majority of them concentrated near the hotel. Inside, the dining room was crowded with equal numbers of guards and astronomers. Almost everyone seemed to be there, and a few shot me sympathetic looks as I was marched by. I didn't see Martine or Carla. I didn't have time to ask any questions because I was whisked quickly into the library.

At the main table were seated two men and a woman. From their attire, it was clear that these were not security grunts. After a moment, the senior officer, an older woman who seemed vaguely familiar, turned to me and asked me to be seated.

"Dr. Alexander, I would like to say that it is a pleasure to see you again, but the circumstances are less than desirable."

I remembered, then, that I did know this woman. Her name was Jonna, Tir Jonna. I had met her at one of Saskia's infrequent dinner parties. She was a colonel in UniTech security. Clearly, I was in deep trouble. The numbness that had set in hours before had started to wear off, and I was beginning to feel truly afraid.

"Where is Martine Gerra?" one of the men snapped abruptly.

I was pleased that I was able to keep from jumping at the sound of his angry voice, but his question had startled me. Had Martine escaped somehow? Or were they testing me? In either case, the less said, the better.

"Dr. Gerra and I went for a walk earlier this morning," I said as smoothly as possible. "I sat down for a rest and she continued on. I haven't seen her since."

"A sixty-five-year-old woman continued hiking when you had to rest?" the other man sneered disbelievingly.

The two men were nearly identical. Same cropped hair, blunt chin, belligerent voice. Only a slight difference in hair and eye color established them as distinct individuals. From their insignia, I deduced that they were captains.

"It takes time to adjust to the thin air up here," I said mildly. "Dr. Gerra has been here for some time, and I only just arrived. Age makes little difference."

I have always been proud of my ability to remain calm even when I'm terrified. I would get hysterical later. At the moment, though, I remained detached enough to recognize and analyze the aggressive questioning tactics without taking it personally.

"Enough," Colonel Jonna said softly, calling off the dogs for the moment. "Now, Dr. Alexander, I'm sure you must have some idea why we are here."

I nodded, but I was puzzled nonetheless. UniTech's role in this business was a mystery to me, although it was clear I had stumbled into something big and ugly.

"You have been charged with a serious crime, for which the penalty is quite severe. This investigation is designed to give you every opportunity to explain your actions."

"What, exactly, are the charges against me?" I asked carefully.

One of the indistinguishable captains snorted and crossed his arms, but Jonna answered my question politely enough.

"Conspiracy to sabotage the Net," she said.

I looked at her in amazement. Astronomy, I had expected. Even illegal entry into the Net. But sabotage? Stars above, where had they gotten that one?

"Could you explain that to me?" I asked finally.

"In the last week, there have been two illegal entries into the Net from this point of origin. At the time of the first entry, a malicious and destructive computer code was introduced. It was necessary to freeze the Net for twenty-four hours and reboot the entire system from scratch in order to eradicate the code. On the second entry, the culprit was g-identified via her IMC as Dr. Quincy Alexander. The destructive code was again introduced, and another freeze was necessary before the Net was functional again."

I was so surprised, I couldn't say anything.

"We know you did an integrity check on Saskia's files," Colonel Jonna said. "You were making sure you'd destroyed her work, weren't you?"

"No!" I cried. "You've got it all wrong. That's not what happened."

"What was it?" the captain on the left injected. "Jealousy? Rage? Revenge?"

"None of those." I was thoroughly exasperated. "Hasn't anyone told you? We had the same problem. Saskia's work was disintegrating. We couldn't stop it."

"A convicted Net criminal, Patrique Grec, has confessed to abetting you," the other captain said.

"Abetting nothing, Patrique was trying to get help," I said. "We needed to back-up the library, and we didn't have enough tapes."

"And the code conveniently leaked through when he entered," Jonna finished for me.

"That might have happened," I admitted. "I had no idea that the problem was mobile."

Actually, I should have thought of it. The decompressor was self-programming and auto-updating. If it sensed an outdated version at the other end of the connection, then it would automatically send a replica of itself to replace it. That's what it must have done.

"Sure you didn't," one of the men said.

I decided not to bother keeping the two of them straight. They were condescending assholes, and I wanted to pop both of them.

"It might have been an accident on Patrique's part," he continued, "but not on yours. You knew that the killer code would go through, didn't you? You made it that way."

"There isn't any killer—"

He cut me off.

"That's not what Patrique said. You set that poor sucker up, didn't you? You figured that since he'd already been nailed as a Net criminal once, the blame would naturally fall on him again."

I stared at him in disbelief.

"Patrique said that?"

The man turned to Jonna. She nodded once.

"Bring him in," she ordered.

There was silence until the captain returned with Patrique in tow. Patrique looked like shit. He hadn't shaven, and his clothes were in disarray. His eyes had a haunted look.

"I'm sorry, Quincy," he said, his voice quivering with misery.

Clearly, he'd been through a lot this morning. UniTech security must have dragged him out of bed and questioned him for hours. It didn't look like they'd actually tortured him, at least not physically, but UniTech had once taken everything away from him, and now they were threatening what little life he'd scraped together out here at La Vista.

"What for?" I asked gently.

"It's just that it all started when you got here," he said without meeting my eye. "Everything was fine until you arrived, and then suddenly there's this problem."

He really thought that I'd done it. It wasn't too hard to understand, I suppose. UniTech was here, questioning us, so they couldn't have done it. Ergo, I was the next best culprit. I stared at him sadly. That he had failed to trust me did not surprise me. After all, I hardly knew him. Still, it hurt that he believed the lies these thugs had fed him. They were trying to demoralize me by showing me how my friends turned against me, but all they were succeeding in doing was pissing me off.

At another nod from Jonna, the man got up and led Patrique out of the library. When they were gone, I turned back to Jonna, angry enough not to watch my tongue.

"What did you do to him?" I asked. "Hasn't he been hurt enough by you people? You stripped him of everything once, now you've come back to haunt him."

Jonna just shook her head.

"I'll do what needs to be done to get to the bottom of this," she said.

I wasn't sure what to make of the strained note in her voice. Was it possible she had some compassion for Patrique?

"In any case, your cooperation will, in part, determine how long this investigation will be prolonged. The sooner we find out who was involved in this sabotage, the sooner we can all go home."

"But there was no sabotage," I said. "If you would just listen to me, I can explain. Nobody created anything. It was an accident. If you have to blame somebody, blame Saskia. It's her own fault."

I finally had Jonna's attention.

"Explain," she said.

So I did. I left out Rubie—I would have to think about her later—but I described everything else. I went through the old version of the decompressor and showed her the bug. I ran my simulations for her. I was even able to show how the auto-updating feature on the decompressor would account for all the invasions of the Net.

It was hard to tell, but I think that Jonna believed me. She sat for a few moments, staring off into nothing. I realized that Jonna, along with all the other guards, had to have an inner ear radio. Whenever they appeared to be gazing into space, they were actually listening to reports. I could also just barely hear Jonna growling ever so softly in her throat. That meant she also had a vocal cord transmitter through which she could send orders without having to speak out loud. No wonder the whole operation moved so seamlessly.

"All right," she said to me, "you may go. Your arguments have been most convincing. I will take them under consideration."

I made for the door, almost swimming in relief.

"Ah, Dr. Alexander. I have one more question."

I turned slowly.

"Yes?"

Colonel Jonna steepled her fingers. She looked preoccupied, but I knew better than to be fooled by that.

"Do you," she asked, "happen to know the present whereabouts of Dr. Rubie Marle?"

Dr. Rubie Marle? It was an effort, but I kept my face absolutely expressionless. So much for the climbing bum act. I had started to suspect that she was hiding something like that.

"I don't know," I said, which seemed like a safe thing.

"You don't know?" the remaining captain said. It seemed that derision was the only emotion he was capable of. "You've been fucking her for a week and you have no idea where she is?"

So they knew that much. I was getting frightened. How much

more did they know about Rubie? Not enough, I prayed, to make them as suspicious of her as I was.

"No, actually, I have no idea at all," I said firmly. "She left on a camping trip yesterday. Said she'd be back in a week or so."

"Why wasn't she here helping you with your computer problem?" Jonna asked. "She is, after all, one of the best numerical simulators on the Net."

I shrugged. It was a very good question, one that I wanted an answer to myself.

"She wasn't actually at La Vista very often," I said. "I don't think she was aware of the details or the extent of the problem. I never discussed it with her, at any rate."

"Didn't talk much outside of bed, eh?" Jonna commented.

I gave her a surprised look. Was she joking with or insulting me?

"Look here," I said, bringing my hand down on the table firmly, acting like the aggrieved and protective lover I was. "Rubie hasn't done anything wrong. She's on vacation. She just came here to climb. She's not an astronomer."

Jonna blinked.

"I'm aware of that, Dr. Alexander," she said. "I wasn't insinuating anything of the sort."

"So what do you want with her?" I asked.

My jaw was almost locked with anxiety, but I managed to get the words out. Jonna just looked at me for a moment. She sighed. I held my breath.

"Dr. Marle's model of global weather patterns turned out to be much more accurate than previously thought. Certain rewards are, of course, in order. Her science administrator was hoping that she'd consider cutting her sabbatical short and return to work on the project. I am only his messenger."

Slowly, I let my breath out. Jonna did not appear to have connected Rubie with the computer business, nor did she seem to know about Rubie's feelings for Saskia. This was good. There was trouble there, I knew it. I filed away Jonna's message. Weather modeling? Heavens. At least now I knew why all Rubie's weather forecasts were dead on.

Sergeant Fawks returned to take me to my quarters. As we passed into the hallway, I saw Martine being led down by another guard. I longed to say something to her, but it was impossible. She threw me a reassuring glance before disappearing into the library. I felt better. Somehow, I knew she would say the right things, telling the truth as necessary, but leaving out the things that nobody was supposed to know.

Back in my quarters, I stripped and lay down to sleep. Several minutes later I got up and put my clothes on again. Things seemed calm for the moment, but if those guards came bursting through my door at some odd hour, I didn't want to be sleeping naked. I settled back against the pillows. I was so tired. I thought I would fall asleep immediately, but I didn't. My body grew incredibly heavy, and I couldn't keep my eyelids open, but my mind was still racing. I turned over the events of the day at random, like they were shells on the beach, and I marveled again at all the wonder and horrors therein. I tried to make sense out of it, but it seemed chaotic in spite of my efforts. Saskia had deceived me at every level. It was a tremendous blow. But the person to whom my thoughts constantly returned was Rubie, not Saskia. She had lied to me, too. How did she fit in to this mess? I feared the worst.

10

I awoke with a start the next morning. I looked around, half-expecting UniTech security guards to be tearing my room apart. There was no one. Everything was peaceful. The sun was just peeking into my window. That must have been what roused me. I hadn't woken up to sunshine in many days. I'd forgotten to put my light-tight shades down the night before. I guessed that it didn't really matter. What was the use of minimizing light pollution when we couldn't observe?

Although I was full of nervous energy, I wasn't yet ready to face UniTech. I considered stretching out but decided against it. I was too restless to relax into it and would probably pull a muscle if I tried. I resorted to prowling around the room.

As I paced past my desk, I noticed something I hadn't seen the night before. A blue iris. I picked it up. It must have been sitting there for a while since the ends of the petals were already curling up, dry and brown. It had to have come from the greenhouse—I remembered admiring a patch of them there—but how did it get onto my desk?

Who else but Rubie would have put it there? I bit my lip and sat down on the bed. Ever since Martine told me that she'd left to go hiking, I'd been scared shitless that maybe Rubie would do what Cass had done: walk out of my life without a word. Rubie hadn't left a note either, but she had left me a flower. Of course, it would have been nice if she'd taken the time to post me a little message. She'd probably been pretty distressed about the g-ID correlation at the time, though. If I'd been in her position, I wouldn't have had the presence of mind to write a note either. The iris was a good sign. It meant she was coming back. It had to mean that.

"Just don't come back too soon," I muttered, shaking the bruised flower a little, "because UniTech will string you up by the toenails if they start thinking what I'm thinking."

I, of course, intended to shake her silly when she returned, but that was nothing compared to what UniTech would do.

My thoughts were interrupted by a knock at the door. A knock. Well, that was civilized. I put the flower down and answered it. It was Sergeant Fawks. She looked as fresh and cheerful as ever, although I suspected that she'd been standing outside my door for most of the night. Her first name, I discovered, was Elli, and she didn't seem to mind me calling her that.

First, we went to the showers. Elli courteously waited outside while I bathed and dressed. We went to the dining hall next, and Elli drank coffee while I bolted down some breakfast. The guards had taken over the kitchen and managed to produce an edible bowl of oatmeal and not-too-soggy toast. A few astronomers sat several tables away, but I was not allowed to speak with them.

After breakfast, Elli did not take me back to my quarters. She directed me instead to the library, where Jonna had apparently set up her headquarters. Elli dropped me off and left. Patrique, Carla, and Martine were already there.

"So," Jonna said, as soon as I was seated, "all the important players are here."

For some reason, that sounded ominous. I wasn't sure I liked being a player in an unknown game for unknown stakes. On the other hand, I was relieved. Rubie Marle was not on Jonna's list of important people. That meant she was safely insignificant. I just hoped she had enough sense to stay clear until things straightened out.

"What exactly is going on here?" Patrique asked bluntly.

He looked slightly less miserable than he had the day before. He looked, I realized after a second, resigned.

"I have examined Dr. Alexander's work and have found that the computer code was indeed spawned by a bug in Rushkin's decompressor protocol. It was, most probably, completely unintentional. The charges of conspiracy and sabotage will be dropped."

I let out a sigh of relief. Perhaps my faith in UniTech was not completely unfounded.

"However..."

My heart sank. Of course, there would be a however.

"...there is this issue of La Vista itself. You have, unfortunately, put yourselves on the map again with this little incident. A working observatory with a connection to the Net."

"Everybody here is a volunteer, and we have never used the Net for anything but emergencies," Patrique shot in. "We don't even get MedCen updates."

Jonna held up her hand.

"I know, I know. And I believe you. But some people don't. My boss, for example. He's wondering why there's so much hardware lying around that could be put to use for the Reconstruction."

"Come on, Tir," Martine said with a familiarity that made me think they were old acquaintances, "everything here has been outdated for decades. What's UniTech going to do with it? It's junk."

Jonna got up and walked over to the window. The view was as spectacular as ever, but I couldn't appreciate it.

"Martine, you and I both know that UniTech has no use for anything at La Vista. But that computer code caused a crisis on the Net. It was degenerative and contagious—some people were saying a virus had invaded the electronic realm. There were all sorts of prophecies: the Fourth Catastrophe, the demise of UniTech, the end of humanity. UniTech's computer technicians were working around the clock to clean the system. The effort and expense involved were truly astounding. You have explained everything satisfactorily, but people are still frantic. After something like that, La Vista can no longer simply be ignored."

"Are you going to arrest us?" Carla asked quietly.

I saw her reach for Patrique's hand. Certainly, he had the most to lose. He'd already been convicted once. I wondered what they'd do to him a second time.

"No," Jonna said with a heavy sigh. "I'm afraid it's much worse than that. I've been ordered to shut this place down. Remove anything remotely functional, from the power generator to the library computer."

I closed my eyes. It was worse than being arrested. The second death of La Vista, the end of astronomy.

"What good will that do?" Martine asked, wearily.

"Prevent things like this from happening again," Jonna replied.

"Then just take away the Net patch-in," Patrique cried. "You don't have to shut it all down."

My heart went out to him. This was, after all, his home. I doubted that there was any way that he could live without the scopes, much less the water pump, the power generator, the greenhouse. Certainly, there was nothing left for him at UniTech. If he went back, he'd be assigned a dead-end, low-level job. He'd die of boredom.

"No, Dr. Grec," Jonna said, "it's just not enough. The bureaucrats are panicked. They won't be appeased by half-measures. They want the guts of this place."

"This is not some star-cursed power trip," I said, finally frustrated enough to speak up. "We're talking about these people's lives. We're talking about an endeavor that has been going on for thousands of years. And you want to kill it? Erase the life's work of countless astronomers? It's not like we're asking for a whole hell of a lot. Take your Net and leave us alone."

Jonna stood there, looking out, shaking her head. When she turned around, she met my eyes, and I saw something like sympathy there.

"Please believe me, Dr. Alexander," she said. "I would if I could. It's not my decision. It's out of my hands. And the people who do make the decisions are frightened. They fear astronomy almost as much as the virals. The space race, nuclear missiles—that's how they think of astronomy."

Unfortunately, I did believe her. I knew that appealing to her would not work. I sank back in my chair. Jonna continued to talk, this time about evacuation plans, but I no longer listened. I looked around the room. My gaze passed quickly over Patrique, his face so stricken that it was painful to watch. Martine and Carla just looked tired and, I was shocked to see, old.

Everyone was standing up. Apparently, the meeting was over. The evacuation was set to begin tomorrow at dawn. I left the room behind the others.

I had gotten five steps when I realized that Elli had not followed me down the hallway. I turned back around. She was standing at the doorway.

"Aren't you supposed to be following me?" I asked.

"The colonel took me off," she said cheerfully. "You're free to go."

"Oh," I said and walked away.

I wandered into the dining room. The guards were gone, and many of the astronomers had gathered there. Martine and Carla were in the middle of them, quietly explaining what had transpired earlier. They emphasized the need to evacuate in groups, to pack out as much data as we could. Even if UniTech did not outright destroy all the information, anything left unattended at La Vista would soon fall prey to the harsh desert weather. Some faces wore looks of disbelief, but many more were stained by tears. Miserable as I was, I did not want company at the moment, so I kept to the walls, trying to pass by unnoticed. Martine caught my eye as I edged by. For a moment, I feared she would drag me into the plans, but she just gave me a tiny nod of understanding and glanced away.

The air was cold. The gray clouds moving in from the east hinted at snow. I thrust my hands deep in my pants pockets and shivered. The flashes of sunlight in between the cloudy patches did nothing to warm me. Mostly to keep warm, I started walking to the scopes.

The giant white domes stood as immovable and unperturbed as they had been on the day I arrived. I smiled a little at the memory of those first astounding hours at La Vista, the glory and the wonder I felt when I rested my hand against the smooth white columns. The scopes had reminded me then of a forest of fungi. Not any more. Now I looked on them as a herd of magical beasts, white giants of infinite patience and calm. And UniTech was going to kill them, rip out all their computer brains and shatter their mirror eyes. No more would they gaze serenely on the night sky. I felt like I was watching an old friend die. Another one. The fierce, chill wind whipped across my face.

As I rounded the last scope before the solarscope, I was struck by an incredible sense of déjà vu. There was Patrique, hunched over the solarscope mirror, just as he had been on the day I first saw him.

I approached quietly. Patrique was working frantically, unscrewing the mirror from its mount. I stood ten feet off, watching as he carefully wrapped the mirror in cloth and tucked it into a box. When there was no chance of him dropping and breaking anything, I called out.

Patrique spun around, his eyes wild with fear.

"It's just me, Patrique," I shouted over the howl of the wind.

For a moment I wondered if that would be reassuring to him at all, considering his earlier suspicions. But he seemed to have forgotten his doubts of me, because he gathered up his mirror and motioned me inside the tiny shack that housed the computers for the solarscope.

"I'm going to save the solarscope," he said, when the door was shut to the wind. "It's small and simple enough. Just this mirror and those two racks of electronics. I can dig a hole on the other side of the NTS and bury them. When UniTech clears out, I can come back and set it up again."

It just might work. The solarscope's main components could be moved in half a dozen trips. The only real problem I saw was that dirt and snow would wreak havoc with those delicate electronic pieces.

"Can't be helped," Patrique said, when I voiced my fears. "I have to do something tonight. This is the best I can think of. It would be great if we had a secret hiding place, but we don't. If Rubie were here, she might know of some nearby caves or something. I'll just have to make do without her, though."

I suddenly realized that I knew of a dry, well-protected cave on the lee side of the mountain—the perfect place to store this equipment. I told Patrique, and was rewarded with a flood of gratitude. We decided it would be best to move under the cover of darkness. After spending another hour carefully packing away the electronics, we agreed to meet again after sunset. With both of us carrying, it would take three trips at most.

Patrique returned to the hotel in comparatively good spirits while I continued my stroll around the scopes. The cave underneath the NTS would provide an excellent hiding place for Patrique and any equipment we could haul there. I was glad I would be able to save one small part of La Vista, but now I had a new worry: what was I going to do about all the other stuff stored inside the cave? Martine had made it clear that she wanted nothing more to do with it. Those embryos had become my responsibility.

Forget about it. That was my first thought. *It's disgusting. An abomination. Let it rot.* But it was hard to maintain that stance for long. Saskia's attitude toward clones was reprehensible, but the embryos themselves were innocent. Those frozen cells represented the possibility of human life. Humanity had far too fragile a hold on existence for me to dismiss the potential stored in that cave. Besides, they were incredibly valuable. Here were half a million completely new and original genetic codes. There was no telling what MedCen could do with them. Maybe they would develop new splicing techniques for cloning. Anything was possible. But the power generators were going to be shut off tomorrow. Then the freezers would defrost and everything would be lost.

Oh, Saskia, I thought for the hundredth time that day. She had really gotten me into a mess. Everything, I thought ungenerously, was her fault.

At that moment I had a revelation so intense, it sent tingles down my spine. Saskia may have been the cause of my problems, but she was also the heart of the solution. I turned around and headed for the hotel at a run. I knew exactly what I had to do.

★

I nearly bowled over Patrique in the kitchen.

"Don't do anything until you hear from me," I hissed as I pulled him to his feet. "I've got an idea."

I was moving again before he could respond. I strode through the dining room and went right up to the two guards blocking the entry to the library. One of them was Elli.

"I must speak to the colonel," I said to her.

"She is in an important meeting, Dr. Alexander," Elli said politely, but firmly. "Come back another time."

"You don't understand," I said, moving to push by her. "This is extremely urgent."

Of course, I didn't get past Elli. She easily immobilized me with her usual cheerful firmness. I hadn't expected to actually get into the library that way, but I had wanted to let Elli know how important my message was.

"Why don't you tell me what it is," Elli said, restoring me to my feet much farther away from the library door, "and I'll pass it along when the colonel is free?"

I studied Elli's calm face. She couldn't have been more than twenty-five years old. A clone, I realized suddenly. She must have been. I found myself wondering if her predecessor had been as smooth and strong as she was.

"Tell her," I said, choosing my words carefully, "that I wish to discuss the long-term side effects of IMCs."

Elli gave me an odd look.

"Just tell her that," I said, turning away. "I'll be in my quarters when she wants to talk to me."

I don't know why, but I trusted that Elli would pass along my message. I thought she liked me enough to do me this one small favor. I went to my room and took a nap.

It was almost dinnertime before Elli came to get me.

"Colonel Jonna will see you now," she said, clearly puzzled by this fact.

So my message had been delivered. I ran my fingers through my hair and straightened my clothes.

"Thanks, Elli," I said. "I'm ready."

Elli led the way to the library. I could tell that she was curious about how I'd managed to swing this interview, but she was too well disciplined to pry. She let me into the room and closed the door behind me. The goon captains were gone. There was no one in the library except me and Jonna. She was staring out the window again, her back to me. I cleared my throat to get her attention, although I was sure she knew I was there. She turned.

"Will you join me in a glass of wine?" Jonna asked quietly.

I assented. She poured. The bottle was of Chilean vintage, many, many decades old. I wondered if it was part of Patrique's storehouse.

"Yes," Jonna said, in answer to my question, "it's from here, of course. There are many hidden treasures at La Vista."

I took the glass, but I couldn't drink it. It represented just one more way that UniTech was plundering La Vista. Jonna drank in silence for a few moments.

"So," she said, finally, "you wished to see me. An urgent matter, I believe."

"I have a proposal."

"Indeed. What are you proposing?"

"An exchange."

"And you want?"

"La Vista," I said promptly. "Leave the equipment as it is, pretend you never saw us."

Jonna shook her head, a sad smile flitting across her face.

"I told you. I don't have the authority. There's nothing you could give me that would make me do it. I'm bribe-proof."

"This is not a personal proposal," I said sharply. "I'm speaking to you as a representative of UniTech."

"But I'm afraid you don't have anything that UniTech wants. Or can't have," she said, lifting the bottle to refill her glass.

It was time to address the matter directly.

"Have they cloned you yet?" I asked.

Jonna's hand jerked slightly, spilling a few drops of wine on the table. She recovered quickly, filling the glass with a steady hand.

"More?" she asked. "Ah, I see you haven't been drinking. Perhaps you prefer white."

I ignored the distraction.

"Smart, sturdy, unflappable. A healthy body, good teeth. I'd be surprised if they haven't made three or four of you already."

Jonna lifted her glass and studied the refraction of light through the red liquid. I held my breath.

"There is only one that I know of," she said finally, her eyes sad and distant.

She drained her glass and filled it again.

"I was not aware that Dr. Rushkin was wont to tell her subordinates so much," she continued. "Of all the UniTech administrators, she was always the most vehement about the need for secrecy."

I shrugged. Jonna was assuming that Saskia had let me know about the clones, and I was not about to dispute it. Martine and Rubie would remain safely out of this discussion.

"How much did she tell you?" Jonna asked, her eyes narrowing on my face.

"Enough," I said, with yet another shrug. "A world full of clones, a species that can no longer reproduce without gene engineering and birthing labs, a propaganda machine of frightening proportions."

"So it's blackmail, is it?" Jonna asked, leaping ahead of me. "Silence is your part of the exchange. If we don't leave La Vista alone, you'll blab the secret, stir what's left of the human race into a panic."

I shook my head. I wasn't that much of a fool.

"Hardly. We both know that UniTech has much more efficient ways of enforcing my silence. An unfortunate accident in the evacuation, perhaps."

The pained look that Jonna gave me told me it was true. I wondered why she was in this job when she had such an obvious distaste for the necessary duties of a security officer.

"I'll do what's necessary," she murmured into her glass.

"Well, I won't make it necessary for you to off me," I said with false levity. "My proposal is much more civilized."

Jonna gestured for me to continue. There was a slight lift in the heaviness of her eyes. If I hadn't known better, I would've thought she wanted me to win this exchange.

"Saskia had a well-known aversion to clones. The thought, in fact, downright disgusted her, and the possibility that they would inherit the earth threw her into fits of nausea. Now suppose, just suppose, she decided to take matters into her own hands. What if she decided to appropriate some of the last viable embryos and freeze them until the day that humans could live in unbridled fertility?"

Jonna sat straight up.

"Then it's not just a fairy tale," she exclaimed. "All those rumors about Rushkin's baby cache. They're true!"

"Hold on," I said, raising my hand. "I didn't say any of it was true. This is all just a supposition."

Jonna swept my words aside with a wave of her arm.

"It's here at La Vista, isn't it? Tell me where," she demanded.

She got to her feet, ready, I'm sure, to start searching that very moment. I leaned back in my chair, finally feeling in control of the situation.

"I was speaking of an exchange," I said quietly.

★

It took Jonna less than twenty minutes to establish a satellite tele-conference with her direct superior, Saul Mitchel, Director of Security. I ate dinner while she explained my proposal to him. I was called back into the library a short while later. I took a seat next to Jonna and across the table from a full-size hologram of a tall, graying man with enormous jowls. He launched into the discussion with no pre-liminaries.

"We'll find it without you," he said belligerently.

This was the dangerous part. It was possible that he was correct. Actually, I was a little surprised that Jonna had not reached the same conclusion. I had anticipated this reaction and planned for it.

"Perhaps," I said mildly. "But probably not before daybreak."

"What happens at daybreak?" Jonna inquired.

"The evacuation begins," I replied, "and the storage chamber will self-destruct."

They both looked at me in horror.

"You wouldn't do that," Mitchel said.

"Why not?" I asked. "I have nothing to lose."

It was all a lie, of course. I wouldn't know an explosive from plum pudding. Still, there was no way they could know that. If I could carry off my story, then they wouldn't be able to test the truth. Therein lay my success.

"And, even if you did find it in time," I added, "you wouldn't get in without blasting. Any attempt to subvert the security system will also cause the contents to self-destruct."

I didn't know if this was entirely true or not, but it sounded good. At any rate, there was enough truth in my words to convince even the arrogant son-of-a-bitch Mitchel. He couldn't risk being wrong.

"Call it off," he said curtly to Jonna.

I looked at Jonna in surprise. She had started a search, anyway. That's where all the guards were. Not quite the advocate I'd thought she was. She gave me an almost apologetic look and growled incoherently into her throat mike. Mitchel turned to address me.

"You'll show us where the embryos are immediately," he said peremptorily.

I raised an eyebrow.

"No, I'm afraid that's not the way it's going to be," I said lazily.

The hologram was remarkably accurate. I could see his face flush red. I continued before he could spout off the angry words forming in his mouth.

"I want all UniTech security removed to the far side of the airfield at the base of the foothills."

"But that's eighty kilometers away!" Jonna said.

"A safe distance," I said. "You will leave me one vehicle and a portable cold storage unit. Tomorrow at dawn, I will drive down and give you the frozen cells."

A lightning look passed between Mitchel and Jonna. If I hadn't been waiting for it, I would have missed it.

"And, just in case you were thinking of arresting me tomorrow, or any of the astronomers at any future time, I would like to inform you that what I bring down will only be a fraction of Saskia's collection. Continued good relations between UniTech and the astronomers of La Vista will ensure regular shipments."

Mitchel was clearly outraged. Jonna looked slightly amused.

"And just how many embryos are we talking about?" he growled.

"In total? Maybe a few thousand. Maybe a few hundred thousand. It's hard to say."

From the looks on their faces, I saw that neither of them had considered a cache of that magnitude. I decided to press on while the advantage was mine.

"La Vista's connection to the Net will remain intact. We won't do astronomy on the Net, but I want open lines of communication. I also want assurances that everyone at La Vista will be allowed to return to their normal jobs at UniTech, no questions asked. Any harassment will result in the immediate suspension of trade."

There were no objections. A few more minor points were worked out, and Mitchel's hologram took itself off. I bid farewell to Jonna and left the library.

I was not as exultant as I expected. The entire session had been a pure adrenaline rush, but now I was coming down. More mundane details pressed upon me. I was exhausted and I stank.

On my way to the showers I ran into Jin-Li.

"Are you finished packing, Quincy? Patrique's looking for you. He wanted some help with something."

I stared at her. My thoughts were creeping along very slowly. It took me a moment to realize that she didn't know.

"The evacuation's off, Jin-Li," I said. "We're not going anywhere."

The look she gave me started off as disbelief and gradually became pity. She patted my arm awkwardly.

"That's okay, Quincy. Just get some rest. We'll take care of everything."

Stars above. She thought I'd lost my mind after all the strain. Or maybe she thought Jonna had tortured me. I started to correct her, then decided to forget about it. She'd find out soon enough, and I was too brain-dead to argue with her.

11

I woke sometime in the wee hours of the morning. The last few days had completely screwed up my sleep schedule. I pulled on my warm clothes and sturdy boots, and assembled my parka, flashlight, and backpack. After a moment's hesitation, I reached into the drawer by my bed, pulled out Maria's diary, and put that in my backpack, too. It would be my good luck charm.

I headed downstairs. On the way past the showers, I splashed a little water on my face and rinsed out my mouth. The dining room was deserted, but there was light in the kitchen. Martine and Carla were sitting there, drinking tea.

"You're off?" Martine asked.

"Thought I'd have a bite to eat first," I said.

Martine turned on some water for tea.

"Are they gone?" I asked, getting out some bread.

"Hours ago," Carla said.

UniTech had obviously not explained their abrupt departure, but I was sure that Martine and Carla had figured it out.

"All gone?"

"Completely," Martine reassured me. "I counted the last guard."

"Good riddance," I said.

"So where is everybody?" I asked.

"At the scopes," Carla replied. "I thought it would be best if we could get back to a normal routine as soon as possible."

After breakfast, Martine asked if she could accompany me part way. She said she needed to stretch her legs. I agreed, wondering what she wanted to talk about.

"Are they really gone?" I asked.

"Yes, I think so," Martine said.

"Nobody knows why?"

"Well, Carla and I do," Martine said mischievously. "A marvelous idea, Quincy, to rid us of two burdens at once. But the others? Not a clue. Jonna simply told us that they'd gotten to the heart of the matter and were satisfied with the innocence and good intentions of everyone involved."

I had to laugh at that.

"They even left an electric jeep for us to use," Martine said. "Very thoughtful of them."

I peered at the gray plastic lump parked near the hotel, praying that it was not difficult to drive.

"Did they leave anything else?"

"Yes, a helium cold thermos. But you're not going to use it."

"Martine, I need a thermos. How else am I going to get—"

"Shhh. Don't speak so loudly. The domes are open. Of course you need a thermos, but the one they left is gigantic. You could never cart that around. Besides it's probably bugged. They're tracking it."

"Fuck her," I said bitterly, thinking of Jonna. Just when I had started to trust her.

"Don't be too hard on her, Quincy. She's got a rotten job. But she's been on our side as much as she possibly can."

I snorted.

"No, I mean it. I've seen Tir at work before. She tempers a lot of the assholes in security. It's a better institution because of her. Anyway, you don't need their thermos. There are several down in the freezer. Saskia used them all the time. They're the silver suitcase-like things in the side closet. The computer will give you detailed instructions on how to remove the embryos from the main storage area. Just query."

Martine had stopped walking.

"Thanks, Martine," I said.

"Be careful," she said, a little gruff. "We can't have you falling down the mountain and breaking your neck at this late stage."

She bid me farewell and turned back down the dark path.

The task before me was straightforward, and I accomplished it without any difficulty. I had decided that twenty thousand embryos would be plenty to start with. That was enough to let them know we had a big supply, but not so much that we wouldn't have more to bargain with later. They fit easily into one of the thermos suitcases I dug out of the closet.

The jeep, I was pleased to discover, was simple to operate. I had no trouble getting it started or learning to steer it. I was heading down the mountain long before first light.

It was a long drive, almost two hours, so I had a lot of time to think. The problem was that there was nothing I really wanted to think about. My past was full of lies, my future uncertain at best. About halfway into the trip I thought of something that didn't cause me pain: Maria. The last entry I had read dealt with her preparations to leave the observatory. I pretended she was sitting beside me now, that I was driving her to meet the airplane that would take her back to Boston. I imagined we talked about her supernova. She told me she was beginning to think that she was a lesbian. It was a soothing fantasy, and the rest of the trip passed quickly.

The drop-off went without a hitch. Jonna came out to meet me on the landing strip. The rest of her force stayed half a kilometer away. I handed her the thermos without ceremony. She took it from me slowly.

"Good luck," she said, sounding as if she really meant it.

I realized then that Jonna was two people: she was Tir, the compassionate woman, and Colonel Jonna of UniTech security. It was the first woman who spoke to me now, and I believed her.

"Thank you."

I turned around to my jeep.

"You could have had so much more," Jonna called after me. "These embryos are priceless, you know that. UniTech would have done anything to get them. Money, promotions, power."

"I got what I want," I said, slipping into the driver's seat.

"La Vista? Why is it so important to you?"

There was no way of explaining it. If she hadn't felt it when she looked up at the stars, she would never understand. I shrugged and started the engine, but Jonna stopped me before I could drive off.

"Want my advice?"

"Sure," I said, surprised at the offer.

"Stay here at La Vista for a while—a year or so. This incident will blow over. There'll be other crises. People will forget. Then if you want to come back and pick up your normal life, you can."

It seemed like very sensible advice.

"Well, thanks."

"And look me up when you come down. I'd like to have dinner with you."

Her grin was just one notch away from being flirtatious. My jaw dropped as Jonna waved to me, hopped in her vehicle, and roared away.

I drove a little ways off and parked. I wanted to be sure the entire security force departed the area. The electric planes took off one by one. Even when they were all gone, I decided to hang out a while to make sure they didn't turn around and come back.

Maria kept returning to my thoughts. I pulled her diary out of my pack and read the last few pages. When I was done, I closed the book and put it aside, feeling a bit melancholy. Maria's last few weeks at La Vista had been miserable. Rebuffing the numerous men who tried to seduce her had made her something of a pariah. She'd become increasingly isolated. Those final pages spoke of intense loneliness. I wished that there was some way I could reach back in time and comfort her.

How different my experiences at La Vista were from hers! I thought about Rubie, Martine, Carla, and Patrique. I was surrounded by people I liked and admired, much more so than I had been back home in New Seattle. My loneliness had started to recede the moment I walked into the observatory. For Maria, though, astronomy was full of sorrow. Nevertheless, her passion for the universe helped her get over the obstacles a woman astronomer faced. I wondered if I would have been so brave, or so passionate.

The rising sun was warm on my face. I must have dozed off, because when I looked again there was a person standing on the airfield, not a hundred meters away. I froze. Perhaps it was a mirage. Then it started to walk toward me. Was I seeing things? Maybe the sun and the stress had warped my mind.

It was definitely no one from La Vista or UniTech. The person wore a long, white, fluttery robe and a huge floppy hat. She had a terrible hunch in her back. Maybe it was Maria's ghost responding to my summons, I thought, only half in jest. But Maria wouldn't wear such an ugly hat or carry that monstrosity of a walking stick.

"Hey," I called out as the figure crept by me.

"Hay is for horses," came the creaky response.

I blinked. I knew what a horse was. I'd seen one in the city zoo, but I didn't see what that had to do with anything.

"Who are you?" I asked, having to raise my voice a little since the person had continued on the road toward La Vista.

"Alicia," she replied without slowing.

I started up the jeep and drove after her.

"What are you doing?" I said when I was beside her.

"Walking," she answered laconically.

"Where are you going?"

"What's it to you? I'm just an old woman going for a walk. Is there a law against that?"

"Well, no," I said, too puzzled to be exasperated. "I just thought that if you were headed to La Vista, I could give you a lift."

The woman stopped walking and looked up at me. I stared at her face in surprise. She was old, probably well over seventy. If she'd come all the way from New Serena, she was one tough bird.

"You're an astronomer?" she asked suspiciously.

"Sure am," I said proudly.

"Huh," she grunted. "So what's the nearest star?"

A quiz? Stars above.

"You mean, besides the Sun?"

Alicia cackled a little. I wondered if she was playing with a full deck.

"Very good. Yes, the next one after the Sun."

"Alpha Centauri."

"And how far away is it?"

"Four and four-tenths light years."

"What's that in parsecs?"

I told her. She grunted, apparently satisfied.

"Very well, then," she said. "I'd love a ride. And on the way, you can tell me how a science criminal like yourself came into possession of a UniTech jeep."

Oh. So it was the jeep that had made her suspicious. I laughed and pulled her into the front seat next to me. The hunch in her back turned out to be a pack very much like mine.

"It's a long story, Alicia."

"Start talking, kiddo. And don't spare me the details."

Alicia already knew about the problem with the library computer. She'd been the one who Patrique had contacted about bringing more storage tapes.

"Well, shit," she said, pulling a stack of the tapes out of her pack. "Do you mean to tell me that I hauled these bricks up here for nothing?"

I reassured her. The tapes would still be useful. If this incident had taught us nothing else, it had shown us how important external back-ups were. That seemed to mollify Alicia.

The story I told her was as much fact as fiction.

"UniTech left us the jeep," I said, "as a gift, a way of apologizing for the inconvenience they'd caused us."

She raised an eyebrow at that, but she didn't question my explanation.

I thoroughly enjoyed the drive back. Alicia was undeniably brusque, and her humor, when I could understand it, bordered on wicked. Still, I found her delightful. She was certainly going to liven things up at the observatory.

Alicia hopped off the jeep before we'd come to a complete stop outside the hotel.

"Gotta check out the scopes," she said. "See you at dinner, kiddo."

She was gone before I could tell her that my name was Quincy. I watched her go, shaking my head a little. La Vista sure did attract some eccentric people. It really wasn't any wonder, though. How many people would risk being an outlaw just to look at the night sky? You'd have to be a little crazy to make the trip. Still, I had to admit that it worked out just fine. The vast machinery that Saskia had set into motion was operating perfectly: astronomers came and went, bringing their talents and skills, taking away the stuff of dreams.

I parked the jeep and went inside. There was no one around. All sleeping, I supposed. Even Patrique was not to be found. I was about to go to my room when I noticed a familiar looking backpack on the floor by the door. It was Rubie's.

I searched the hotel, but could not locate any sign of her. I considered going to the scopes, then dismissed the idea. I was dead tired. Let her find out what had happened from someone else. I stumbled down to my room and into bed.

★

Two hours of nightmares later, I decided to forgo the remainder of my nap. The shadow of Saskia darkened my dreams, denouncing my treachery and chasing me to hell. Rubie was there, too, another shadow of destruction, hot on Saskia's heels. I woke up tangled in bed covers, covered in sweat. My mouth was dry and foul-tasting.

I gathered my things and headed for the showers, hoping to clear some of the filth out of my head as well as off my body. It was after noon, and there was still no one around. Just as well. I wasn't in the mood to chat.

I paused at the mirrors over the sink. I looked terrible. My face was patchy with sleep, my hair was matted on one side. There was probably moss growing on my teeth. I turned on the shower to let it warm up, then I brushed and flossed so vigorously that my gums turned rosy red. I stripped off my clothes and kicked them into a corner. They reeked with the anxiety of the past several hours.

Just as I was about to step into the steaming water, I realized that I'd left my towel out by the sinks. I opened the door to get it, only to see Rubie standing in front of the mirrors, washing her hands. She must have seen my reflection, because she turned slowly to greet me. The grave look on her face told me my worst suspicions were true— and that she knew I knew the truth. I was speechless. There I was, absolutely furious with her, feeling totally ridiculous because I was stark naked. I reached over and grabbed my towel and retreated back into the shower room.

She followed me. I expected that. What I didn't expect was that she would follow me right into the spray of water. She was still dressed in her hiking shorts and shirt. I stared at her, astonished, as she stood motionlessly beneath the showerhead. She closed her eyes and let the steaming hot water run down her face and body.

"I'm sorry, Quincy," was all she said.

She slid down the wall and sat on the shower floor, completely drenched. After a moment, I reached over and turned off the water. I wrapped myself up in the towel and sat on the stool just outside the stall.

"I wanted her to know," she said, and I knew she was referring to Saskia, "how it felt to have a little bit of poison in your system, just a little something eating away at your innards day after day."

Rubie stopped speaking. I prompted her.

"So you came up here and sabotaged the system. You're good with computers, you made it look like a flaw in the decompressor software. Nobody would suspect you because you pretended to be techno-illiterate."

Rubie nodded and picked up where I stopped.

"I came up a month before she was due to arrive and input the changes. It wasn't much—just enough to get her to pay attention. She wrote the software herself. She'd have found the problem quickly enough, but not before she'd acknowledged my existence. I was going to make her notice me."

"But she died, Rubie! She wasn't going to notice anything. Why didn't you stop it then?"

"I don't know!" Rubie cried. "I don't know. Things just started to get out of hand, and I didn't know what to do."

"I know," I said, unable to keep the bitterness out of my voice. "It was revenge. You couldn't get back at her, so you destroyed her work. You got back at me."

"Quincy, please. Yes, it's true, I didn't give a damn about her work, and at first I hated you because you were so close to her. But then I got to know you, and I almost, I mean, I thought I was falling in love. That's why I told you how to fix it. I hated to see you so hurt. Please believe me."

I couldn't doubt the sincerity of this plea. Whatever else, I was sure that Rubie cared about me. That helped a lot. I reached out my hand, and she took it with both of hers.

"I was so stupid," Rubie continued, clearly miserable. "I had no idea that it would go so far. I had no idea that La Vista would be endangered by my immature little prank or that UniTech would get involved. Stars, Quincy, when Patrique told me what happened, I almost died. If I'd only been here, I could've explained."

"No, Rubie, it's just as well you were off camping," I said. "UniTech wasn't looking for explanations, they were looking for scapegoats. They would have nailed you and then shut down La Vista anyway. I managed to convince them it was an accident."

"You didn't mention me?" she asked.

"Of course not. What good would it have done? Besides, I didn't know for sure. You did an excellent job of making it look like an accident."

Rubie was silent for a while.

"So how did you get them to go away?" she asked finally. "Patrique says you did something."

I bit my lip. Finally, I decided that half the truth was better than none.

"I gave them something they wanted," I said.

I could feel Rubie studying my face.

"And you aren't about to tell me what that something is, are you?" she guessed.

I nodded. Rubie was probably the last person I'd tell. She'd already been hurt enough by Saskia's neglect. I didn't want her to find out that Saskia had loved her less than those frozen embryos.

"It must have cost you dearly," she said with a grimace.

"No," I laughed. "I was glad to be rid of it, actually."

She looked at me in surprise.

"Well, thank you," she said softly.

I looked up and met her lovely, lovely eyes.

"You're welcome."

We were both shivering with cold. I stood up and turned the water back on. Rubie stood up, too, and embraced me under the warm water. We stayed like that until we were both warm. Then I pulled back just enough so that I could unbutton her shirt. Slowly, I peeled it off her breasts and shoulders. I pressed her close to me again, feeling the strong, hard lines of her back under my hands and the soft contours of her breasts against mine. A long, warm time later, I reached between us to unfasten her shorts. I worked to slip them off of her hips, pausing to take her hard red nipples in my mouth before I knelt at her feet.

Rubie handed me the soap, and I lathered my hands slowly. I ran my soapy fingers through her curly pubes, gradually working my way down her lips. I reached up behind her, slipping one hand into her crack. Rubie moved her hips back and forth, gliding on my slick hands. Her little murmurs of pleasure stabbed me in the gut. I looked up for a moment, and the sight of her face, so vulnerable and so intent, made me want to cry and come at the same time.

I had one intensely unnerving moment: this was Saskia's body I was making love to. The woman that I'd been crazy about for years, who'd never let me love her—here she was, reincarnated as a young woman who knew how to love me back. It was incredibly bizarre, but the feeling passed quickly. This wasn't Saskia. It was Rubie in Rubie's body. She wasn't a copy or a parody. She was herself.

The water washed the soap away, and I moved my hands slower and more gently. I leaned in to take her clit on my tongue. My thumb sank into her wet hole as I passed my mouth down one side of her slippery lips and up the other. The flavor of her cunt and the faint hint of lemon soap filled my mouth and throat. My tongue teased and teased. When I felt her start to shake above me, I slowed almost to a stop and let her take her way across my mouth. After she stopped, I pulled her down and kissed her warm, wet face.

There is joy in making love to a woman like that. Wild, thumping, humping sex has its place and pleasures, but tender, unrelenting gentleness is a gift of love.

Rubie opened her eyes, blinking hard. I reached up to wipe her eyes. When she asked what she could do for me, I just smiled and shook my head. That she had taken the gift I offered was euphoric enough. She seemed to understand, because she wrapped her arms around me and held me tight. After a while, we got up and washed each other completely, laughing when the soap slipped through our hands.

12

I announced my intentions to make La Vista my home for a while, and Patrique, Martine, and Carla welcomed me warmly. Patrique withdrew to consult his liquor supplies, already planning a housewarming party.

I passed along Jonna's message about the success of the global weather model, but Rubie informed me that she had no intention of cutting short her year's sabbatical. Her administrator had scorned her model for a long time. She was not about to be taken in by his sudden obsequiousness, nor was she fooled by the promise of rewards. The administrator didn't understand the first thing about her model—he'd just realized that he needed her. Let him sweat, she decided. She was going to frolic in the mountains.

I thought there might be other reasons for Rubie's decision to stay. I hoped that I was one of them. I was pretty sure that I was, but she didn't say anything and I didn't ask.

The truth of her ancestry did not seem to have much of an impact on Rubie as far as I was concerned. In fact, she was hardly bothered by it at all. "It might be different if Saskia were alive," Rubie commented early one evening when she came to wake me up.

Our schedules were reversed: I was always waking up when she was getting ready to wind down. Those few hours when our schedules overlapped and we were both awake at the same time were precious. We were dawn and twilight lovers.

"How so?"

"She's dead, so I'm still the only one of me there is."

"Even if she weren't, you'd still be the only Rubie," I said. "Genes aren't everything. Believe me, you are nothing like her."

"Nothing?"

Suddenly, I remembered green eyes and short tempers and sharp tongues. I pulled Rubie down into bed with me and gave her a big hug.

"Well, hardly anything like her."

We were quiet for a while, each lost in our own thoughts.

"You know," I said finally, "for all her unkindness, Saskia probably did you a favor in the long run."

"How so?" Rubie asked, rolling on top of me.

"You're very different from her, in spite of your g-ID. Perhaps if you'd known her, you would've been more like her. I'm sure you would have absorbed some of her goals, her opinions, her prejudices."

Rubie thought about that one for a while.

"You may be right," she said. "I wanted so much for her to like and acknowledge me. I probably would have ended up imitating her."

"Here's a possible scenario for you. Maybe it wasn't easy for Saskia to ignore you all that time, but she did it because it was in your best interests. She gave you a great gift—the gift of uniqueness."

Rubie was pleased with this explanation. It allowed her to think back on her predecessor with less anger and bitterness. I, too, willed myself to believe what I'd said. I needed that image of Saskia to hold on to. I needed to have a fragment of goodness to remember. Perhaps there was even some truth to it. Perhaps, deep down, it had not been cloning that Saskia had been opposed to, but sameness. Perhaps she hadn't been able to distinguish between the two. If she'd met Rubie, she would've realized that her clone was not her mirror image. Maybe. One could only hope.

In some ways, I was more like Saskia than Rubie was. I had imitated her, deliberately and slavishly, for years. I was getting better, though, even taking an entire week off astronomy to go camping with Rubie. The weather was absolutely beautiful, and I barely regretted not being near a scope. Still, I kept my secrets, just as Saskia had. The nursery—as I had come to think of it—under the NTS was my burden alone. I didn't even discuss it with Martine. I wasn't sure what I would do with it. It was a treasure in some ways, but it made me downright uncomfortable. I tried not to think about it too often.

I read and reread Maria's diary so many times that I feared I would destroy the paper on which it was written. I decided to transcribe it into the library computer and make back-ups on tape so that I would always have a safe copy of it. Rubie teased me about my preoccupation with the diary. She said she'd be jealous if Maria hadn't been dead for so many decades. She was probably right. I was half in love with that astronomer from the past.

There was one passage I had read so often that I had memorized it, every last word and punctuation mark. Still, I loved to open the paper diary and read the looping words. It was a treat I reserved for lonely nights when Rubie was off scaling a distant peak and I was sitting in a cold dome by myself.

> Another equipment failure has halted work on the telescope until tomorrow night. Alone and bored, I try to remember why I am here in this remote and desolate place. I go outside to look at the supernova. It is just visible to the naked eye. War and poverty rock the planet, yet I devote my life to a dot of light in the sky. Is astronomy really worth anything?
>
> Yet I look again at this exploding star. In that burning furnace, new elements come into being. Carbon, oxygen, nitrogen—the elements of life. All the atoms in my body were made inside a star like that. We are born of stars. How could I help but yearn for them? Stardust runs in my veins, urging me skyward.

Our scopes reached out to the night sky, the burning, pulsing cradle of humanity, while deep beneath the NTS another cradle lay, hidden, cold, and quiet. I worked on through the nights, surrounded on all sides by hope and glory.

Skyward.

Other titles from Firebrand Books include:

Artemis In Echo Park, Poetry by Eloise Klein Healy/$8.95
Before Our Eyes, A Novel by Joan Alden/$8.95
Beneath My Heart, Poetry by Janice Gould/$8.95
The Big Mama Stories by Shay Youngblood/$8.95
The Black Back-Ups, Poetry by Kate Rushin/$8.95
A Burst Of Light, Essays by Audre Lorde/$8.95
Cecile, Stories by Ruthann Robson/$8.95
Crime Against Nature, Poetry by Minnie Bruce Pratt/$8.95
Diamonds Are A Dyke's Best Friend by Yvonne Zipter/$9.95
Dykes To Watch Out For, Cartoons by Alison Bechdel/$7.95
Dykes To Watch Out For: The Sequel, Cartoons by Alison Bechdel/$9.95
Exile In The Promised Land, A Memoir by Marcia Freedman/$8.95
Experimental Love, Poetry by Cheryl Clarke/$8.95
Eye Of A Hurricane, Stories by Ruthann Robson/$8.95
The Fires Of Bride, A Novel by Ellen Galford/$8.95
Food & Spirits, Stories by Beth Brant (*Degonwadonti*)/$8.95
Forty-Three Septembers, Essays by Jewelle Gomez/$10.95
Free Ride, A Novel by Marilyn Gayle/$9.95
A Gathering Of Spirit, A Collection by North American Indian Women
    edited by Beth Brant (*Degonwadonti*)/$10.95
Getting Home Alive by Aurora Levins Morales and Rosario Morales/$9.95
The Gilda Stories, A Novel by Jewelle Gomez/$9.95
Good Enough To Eat, A Novel by Lesléa Newman/$8.95
Humid Pitch, Narrative Poetry by Cheryl Clarke/$8.95
Jewish Women's Call For Peace edited by Rita Falbel, Irena Klepfisz, and
    Donna Nevel/$4.95
Jonestown & Other Madness, Poetry by Pat Parker/$7.95
Just Say Yes, A Novel by Judith McDaniel/$9.95
The Land Of Look Behind, Prose and Poetry by Michelle Cliff/$8.95
Legal Tender, A Mystery by Marion Foster/$9.95
Lesbian (Out)law, Survival Under the Rule of Law by Ruthann Robson/$9.95
A Letter To Harvey Milk, Short Stories by Lesléa Newman/$9.95
Letting In The Night, A Novel by Joan Lindau/$8.95
Living As A Lesbian, Poetry by Cheryl Clarke/$7.95
Metamorphosis, Reflections on Recovery by Judith McDaniel/$7.95
Mohawk Trail by Beth Brant (*Degonwadonti*)/$7.95
Moll Cutpurse, A Novel by Ellen Galford/$7.95
The Monarchs Are Flying, A Novel by Marion Foster/$8.95
More Dykes To Watch Out For, Cartoons by Alison Bechdel/$7.95
Movement In Black, Poetry by Pat Parker/$8.95
My Mama's Dead Squirrel, Lesbian Essays on Southern Culture by Mab Segrest/
    $9.95
New, Improved! Dykes To Watch Out For, Cartoons by Alison Bechdel/$8.95
Normal Sex by Linda Smukler/$8.95

Now Poof She Is Gone, Poetry by Wendy Rose/$8.95

The Other Sappho, A Novel by Ellen Frye/$8.95

Out In The World, International Lesbian Organizing by Shelley Anderson/$4.95

Politics Of The Heart, A Lesbian Parenting Anthology edited by Sandra Pollack and Jeanne Vaughn/$12.95

Presenting. . .Sister NoBlues by Hattie Gossett/$8.95

Rebellion, Essays 1980–1991 by Minnie Bruce Pratt/$10.95

Restoring The Color Of Roses by Barrie Jean Borich/$9.95

A Restricted Country by Joan Nestle/$9.95

Running Fiercely Toward A High Thin Sound, A Novel by Judith Katz/$9.95

Sacred Space by Geraldine Hatch Hanon/$9.95

Sanctuary, A Journey by Judith McDaniel/$7.95

Sans Souci, And Other Stories by Dionne Brand/$8.95

Scuttlebutt, A Novel by Jana Williams/$8.95

Shoulders, A Novel by Georgia Cotrell/$9.95

Simple Songs, Stories by Vickie Sears/$8.95

Sister Safety Pin, A Novel by Lorrie Sprecher/$9.95

Skin: Talking About Sex, Class & Literature by Dorothy Allison/$13.95

Spawn Of Dykes To Watch Out For, Cartoons by Alison Bechdel/$9.95

Speaking Dreams, Science Fiction by Severna Park/$9.95

Staying The Distance, A Novel by Franci McMahon/$9.95

Stone Butch Blues, A Novel by Leslie Feinberg/$10.95

The Sun Is Not Merciful, Short Stories by Anna Lee Walters/$8.95

Talking Indian, Reflections on Survival and Writing by Anna Lee Walters/$10.95

Tender Warriors, A Novel by Rachel Guido deVries/$8.95

This Is About Incest by Margaret Randall/$8.95

The Threshing Floor, Short Stories by Barbara Burford/$7.95

Trash, Stories by Dorothy Allison/$9.95

We Say We Love Each Other, Poetry by Minnie Bruce Pratt/$8.95

The Women Who Hate Me, Poetry by Dorothy Allison/$8.95

Words To The Wise, A Writer's Guide to Feminist and Lesbian Periodicals & Publishers by Andrea Fleck Clardy/$5.95

The Worry Girl, Stories from a Childhood by Andrea Freud Loewenstein/$8.95

Yours In Struggle, Three Feminist Perspectives on Anti-Semitism and Racism by Elly Bulkin, Minnie Bruce Pratt, and Barbara Smith/$9.95

You can buy Firebrand titles at your bookstore, or order them directly from the publisher (141 The Commons, Ithaca, New York 14850, 607-272-0000).

Please include $2.00 shipping for the first book and $.50 for each additional book.

A free catalog is available on request.